ONE FOR THE ROAD

After a car accident shatters the lives of Mike and Penny Craven, the ex-racing car driver's morale is low. However, when he sees a young woman attacked by thugs and rescues her, his life begins to take on a new meaning. But soon his courage, his skill as a driver and his marriage are all called into question as he and the young woman face violence and death at the hands of a group of vicious criminals.

PETER CONWAY

ONE FOR THE ROAD

Complete and Unabridged

LINFORD
Leicester

First published in Great Britain by
Robert Hale Limited
London

First Linford Edition
published 2007
by arrangement with
Robert Hale Limited
London

British Library CIP Data

Conway, Peter, *1929 –*
    One for the road.—Large print ed.—
Linford mystery library
    1. Detective and mystery stories
    2. Large type books
    I. Title
    823.9′14 [F]

ISBN 978–1–84617–638–8

Published by
F. A. Thorpe (Publishing)
Anstey, Leicestershire

Set by Words & Graphics Ltd.
Anstey, Leicestershire
Printed and bound in Great Britain by
T. J. International Ltd., Padstow, Cornwall

1

Mike Craven supposed that he ought to have realised what was happening the previous evening — after all, he had had enough practice at it — but Penny had been so near to her old self that he must have shut the possibility right out of his mind. They had had a quiet dinner together, watched an old and rather good film on TV and when they had gone to bed, although nothing had actually happened, he had felt stirrings of emotions that he had thought gone for ever.

The whole business had started again, though, when he woke to find the sun streaming through the window and glancing at the clock, he saw that it was already past nine. It must be those blasted tablets again, he thought, realising with a sudden sense of shock that he had slept through the alarm once more. He sat up abruptly, then fervently wished he hadn't as the room began to spin violently. He waited until the spasm was over and then got cautiously to his feet — if he didn't get a move on, he was going to be late for the interview and he had no doubt in his mind that this one was about his last hope.

Craven knew that it was going to be one of those days as soon as he found the shirt that Penny had promised to iron the previous day, still crumpled up in the wicker basket in the bathroom. About the only thing that could be said for it was that it was clean, but he couldn't put it on like that and ironing shirts most definitely wasn't his line at all.

'Penny! Penny, wake up.'

She burrowed further under the bed-clothes and when he pulled them back, rolled on to her front and buried her head under the pillows.

'Penny, that shirt — I've got to have it within the next ten minutes, otherwise I'll be late.'

When she didn't move, Craven's temper suddenly flared; he snatched up his wife's wooden backed hairbrush and hit her across the back-side. The blow was much harder than he had originally intended and she let out a cry of pain and sat up as if she had been electrocuted.

'You bastard,' she shrieked, her face twisted with hate. 'You spend your whole time hanging around here doing nothing and then you expect me to wait on you hand and foot. Just because you're useless and can't get a job, you take it out on me. You're nothing but a brute; you know I can't stand being hit like that, I don't know why I stay with you . . . ' She burst into tears and when he tried to put his arm around her shoulders, pushed him angrily away. 'Go away,' she screamed, 'I hate you.'

Craven turned wearily towards the dressing table, thinking how unfair it was; it wasn't as if he went in for hitting her — in fact, when he came to think about it, he had never done so before, although in all conscience he had had enough provocation over the years. He plugged his electric razor into the socket at the side of the mirror above the basin and saw Penny rush out of the room, making the floor tremble as she slammed the door.

When he had finished shaving and had done his teeth, Craven looked forlornly at the shirt which was lying on the bed in a crumpled heap and picked it up with a sigh of dismay. How could he expect to impress anyone, let alone a sales manager, if he went along looking as if he had slept on a park bench?

'Mike. Mike, I'm sorry, but you know what I'm like first thing in the morning.' Penny was standing at the door. 'Give it here and I'll have it done for you in no time.'

When she came across and kissed him, Craven picked up the fresh tang of the strong toothpaste she always used and it spoke volumes for the situation they had reached, he thought bitterly, that he should have realised at once what had happened. Penny's behaviour the previous evening, her sudden mood change just now — there was only one possible explanation and only one place where she could have hidden it. It took him less than five minutes to find the nearly empty

4

bottle of vodka in the cistern of the lavatory in the bathroom. Craven sat on the edge of the bath after he had poured the last couple of inches away, feeling utterly defeated.

Penny came at him like an avenging fury when he returned to the bedroom and she saw the bottle in his hand and that it was empty. When he held her wrists to prevent her from scratching his eyes out, she kicked him hard on the shin and it was not until he forced her back on to the bed with his whole weight on top of her that he was able to subdue her. She capitulated quite suddenly, going limp and bursting into floods of tears.

'Is that the only bottle?' She nodded. 'Do you promise me?'

'What else do you want me to do?' she screamed at the top of her voice, 'go down on my knees and beg your forgiveness?'

Craven stretched out his hand towards her, but she pushed it away angrily and buried her head under the pillow. There were so many things he wanted to tell her, but he knew from bitter experience that this would not be the right moment. He put on his crumpled shirt and left without having any breakfast.

★ ★ ★

'I'm sorry, Mr. Craven, I really am, but we were looking for someone younger.'

Craven supposed that he should have been grateful for the fact that the man had put him out of his misery straight away — the usual form was for them to say they'd let him know — but he was a long way past being able to be as dispassionate as that. He tried to keep the note of pleading out of his voice, but even to his own ears, it sounded like a feeble bleat.

'But with my experience . . . '

The man studiously avoided looking at Craven's head and at the same time managed to make it perfectly obvious that he was doing just that.

'We're trying to play down the sporting image at the moment; you'll understand that with the world fuel problems and all that, the larger and faster models are just not selling — and of course we do require our salesman to take our customers out on the road.' He put his hand on Craven's shoulder. 'Don't you think it would be better to try something right away from motoring? I would like to help you, but . . .'

Craven could have told him that he had never done anything else, that he had already attended any number of interviews and that he was fed to the back teeth with receiving gratuitous advice, but he didn't — the man no doubt meant well and even that was beginning to count for a lot. It cost him a mighty effort, but he managed to raise a smile, shook the man by the hand, put on his hat and left.

It took Craven an hour to walk back to his flat and he had ample time in which to reflect on the futility of his efforts to set himself up again and at the same time help Penny. He let out a deep sigh — if the usual pattern was going to repeat itself, she would be full of self recrimination when he got back, which in many ways was even more difficult to bear than her violent moods and verbal assaults.

He knew that there was something seriously wrong directly he opened the door of the flat; there was a sour smell pervading the entrance hall and there was no response to his call. Penny was slumped in one of the armchairs in the living room, her head at an unnatural angle and an empty vodka bottle on the occasional table by her side.

By now, Craven had had enough experience to know that this time she was in a really bad way; the front of her night-dress was stained with vomit, her breathing was shallow and irregular and there was a nasty mauve tinge to her lips. He pulled her down on to the carpet, her limbs flapping about like those of a rag doll, and placed her half on her side, cleaning out her mouth as well as he could with his forefinger and lifting up her chin until her respirations became easier.

Craven sat on the chair by the phone and looked down at his wife for several minutes before dialling the Abbey Nursing Home. He and Penny had been married for fifteen years and to think it had come to this; they had loved one another at one time — they really had — but now there was hate on her side and disgust on his. He let out a weary sigh; he couldn't afford the private clinic, but the psychiatrist there knew the problem, it would save him the ordeal of going through the whole dreary routine of interrogation yet again and he trusted them not to keep her there a day longer than was strictly necessary.

Craven went with her in the ambulance and paced around the waiting room until McAlister, the psychiatrist in charge of her case, had finished his examination.

'Is she going to be all right?'

The elderly Scot had never been one to mince words, which was one of the things Craven liked about him. 'She's not in any immediate danger, if that's what you mean, but this latest relapse coming so soon after the last one is little short of a disaster. She hasn't the will to stop drinking and without that, all the drugs and psychotherapy in the world won't have any lasting effect.'

'But how does one give her the will?'

'If I knew the answer to that one, she wouldn't be lying in there unconscious now. She has some deep underlying guilt feelings that make her despise herself; for her to survive they must be uncovered and that will inevitably take many months of treatment once she is over the acute stage.'

'You have always been straight with me, Dr. McAlister, and I have tried to be the same with you. I have every confidence in your ability, but the truth of the matter is that I can't afford to keep her here for more than another week or two at the most; I haven't been able to find a job and there's precious little money left.'

The psychiatrist raised his hand. 'Don't worry — I know how you're placed. I'll contact my friend Dobson and I'm sure he'll take your wife on as a National Health patient at St. Botolph's Hospital — he runs a unit for alcoholics there.'

'But that's a mental hospital, isn't it? Penny would never agree to go there.'

McAlister put his arm around the other man's shoulders. 'Let's face that one when the time comes, shall we?'

When he got home, Craven did his best to forget his problems and get thoughts of Penny out of his mind. It was a hopeless task; the afternoon dragged by interminably, he couldn't concentrate on the TV, the tins of mince and carrots he had for his supper tasted even more revolting than usual and afterwards, he closed his book after only three pages, getting up from the easy chair and going through into the bedroom, hoping to find relief in sleep.

His anti-convulsant pills, sitting in their small wooden box on the dressing table seemed to mock him as he perched on the side of the bed and started to take off his shoes. It had been the fits that he had had directly before the operation that still prevented him from driving and that had been the main reason for his lack of confidence and inability to get a job. He had been taking the wretched capsules now for just on a year and despite the doctors' warnings, he wasn't going to swallow the damned things any more.

He went through into the bathroom, took the two nearly full bottles out of the medicine cabinet and emptied the contents of both of them into the bowl of the lavatory. As he flushed them away and the last one disappeared, he felt a sense of elation at this gesture of independence, modest though it was. He had felt for some time that the pills had been a great deal to blame for his lethargy and to celebrate his decision to get rid of them, he put on his hat and strode out into the night.

2

Craven had always been fascinated by the back streets of Soho, particularly after dark, and he wandered around for a couple of hours, observing and no doubt being observed by the motley collection of people of all nationalities, shapes and sizes, who populated and were visiting that strange area. He watched the theatre crowds disperse, the clientele of the clubs and restaurants depart and finally all who were left were a few birds of the night, people like himself with nothing else to do and for all he knew, as little left to live for.

He was walking past the entrance to a narrow passage-way when he heard the tattoo of running feet. Glancing to his right, he saw a woman in a white coat only twenty yards away and she caught sight of him almost at the same moment, letting out a despairing cry for help as the two pursuing men caught up with her.

Every instinct he had was shouting at Craven to clear off and mind his own business; in any case, he thought, it was probably only some prostitute trying to welsh on a client. He had even begun to turn away, when he saw the smaller of the two men pinion the woman's arms behind her back and the other one quite deliberately drew back his fist and punched her hard in the stomach. The air was forced out of her lungs, producing an explosive grunt and then she began to retch uncontrollably. Almost against his will, Craven started down the passage and he was only ten feet away when the thug got set to hit her again.

'Leave her alone.'

Craven said it quietly and although it may have sounded cool, the truth of the matter was that his mouth was so dry that he couldn't have spoken any louder to save his life.

Quite slowly, the man let his arm drop to his side and turned round. He was built like a tank, was at least six inches taller than Craven's modest five feet eight and had the sort of features that told of innumerable and largely unsuccessful fights in the ring.

'Well, well, well,' he said with a mocking smile on his battered face. 'What 'ave we 'ere?' He looked Craven up and down and then fixed his gaze on the flat cap, shaking his head in disbelief. 'Why don't you push off, little man? This is none of your business and you don't want to get hurt, now do you?'

'I told you to leave her alone.'

Craven had once done the East African Safari rally with a Swede as navigator, who had at one time in his chequered career been bodyguard to some racketeer and in the plane on the way out there, he had been a constant source of entertainment with his tales of the various nefarious activities he had been involved in and some of the nastier tricks of unarmed combat he had picked up. 'Never try to box a boxer,' he had said, but what else could one do, Craven thought, when a great ape of a man was standing on the balls of his feet, his fists clenched and only a couple of paces away. He had never been in a serious fight in his life and the only trick that Sven had told him about and seemed remotely feasible for someone in his condition meant getting a lot closer.

'Don't hit me, please don't hit me — I've not been well, it's my heart.'

Craven tried to make his voice sound as feeble and shaky as possible, which was not exactly difficult as he was scared out of his wits. He put his arms out sideways in what he fondly hoped would be taken as a pleading gesture and edged gradually towards his assailant. The man's great hands shot out, grasped his victim by the neck and steadily began to squeeze. Craven could hear the roaring beginning in his ears, his arms fluttered higher and cupping his hands, he hit the man across both his cauliflower ears with all the strength he possessed.

Sven had told him that one could easily kill a man by doing that, but he hadn't really believed him. Now, he did. At one moment, the man was standing towering over him and throttling the life out of him and the next, he had dropped to the ground without a sound and lay in a crumpled heap at his feet. Craven stepped over the prostrate figure and faced the second man who was still holding the woman's arms behind her back, staring at the scene with open-mouthed horror.

'How about letting her go now?'

The man backed away until he hit the wooden hoarding and then started to edge sideways.

'I shouldn't leave your friend if I were you — he doesn't look too well.' The young woman was still bending over, massaging her stomach. 'Can you walk?' he asked.

She nodded and Craven took her arm and helped her out of the passage-way and into the street. Reaction hit him when they had gone no further than a hundred yards and he gradually slowed to a halt, beginning to shake uncontrollably.

'Are you O.K.?' the woman asked anxiously.

'Not really. I'm sorry to be so feeble, but I'm not used to this sort of thing.'

'You could have fooled me.' There was the ghost of a smile on her face, which wasn't bad, Craven thought, considering what she had just been through. 'You'd better come up to my flat, I only live about a quarter of an hour's walk away. Do you think you can make that all right?'

'Just about.'

Craven had got some sort of control over himself by the time they got there, enough that is to remember that she was the one who had been hit and to ask her how she felt.

She rubbed her stomach reflectively. 'There's nothing wrong that a stiff brandy and a hot bath won't cure. What can I get you? I've got brandy or whisky.'

'I'd much prefer a cup of tea, if that wouldn't be too much trouble.'

The woman turned away quickly, but not so quickly that he failed to notice the half raised eyebrows and the quizzical smile. He realised now what a mistake it had been to come, but he had felt desperately shaky in the street and he also hadn't known how to refuse without sounding rude and uncaring; another example, he thought bitterly, of just how insecure he had become. He reckoned he would probably have been able to cope with the sort of emotional scene he would have predicted in the case of most ordinary young women who had been through an experience like that, but her complete self possession made him feel more than usually inadequate.

He watched her carefully when she returned with the tea tray and he could have sworn that it wasn't just an act; she was as cool and calm as if she had just been to the theatre. Already he could feel the muscles at the back of his neck beginning to tighten up and as soon as he decently could he got up to go, thinking that other people's troubles were something he could do without, although instinctively he knew that she probably wouldn't be the sort of person to unburden herself to a complete stranger.

'At least you'll let me run you home — my car's in the basement garage. It's the least I can do.'

'No, thanks all the same. It's very kind of you, but it's not far to walk and the fresh air will help to clear my head.'

19

She handed him his cap at the door. 'It was very brave of you to have come to my aid like that — there aren't many people who would have done under those circumstances. I'm very grateful.'

'I'm sorry I made such a stupid exhibition of myself afterwards,' he mumbled stupidly.

Immediately he had spoken he regretted it. He was sure that she had noticed his head — she would have to have been half blind not to — and he dreaded the inevitable questions which were bound to follow. If only he had kept his stupid mouth shut and left while the going was good, he might have got away without the usual inquisition. To his great surprise and even greater relief, she ignored his remark completely and held out a thin strip of paste-board as she opened the door for him.

'Come to lunch or dinner one day soon and then I can say thank you properly; I run a small restaurant quite near to that place where you came to help me.'

Before he had time to think up a reply, she kissed him quickly on the cheek and he was left standing feeling foolish in the corridor.

* * *

In fact, it took Craven a good hour to walk back to his flat and in that time he realised what wonders having been able to deal with the great ape who had attacked the young woman had done for his morale. For the first time since the accident he was able to look at the situation clearly and without self-pity. It was obvious to him that he had made any number of mistakes, but the biggest was undoubtedly refusing to have had his head dealt with properly months ago.

The accident that was to change his life so completely had happened ironically enough, not on the race track, but on their way back from Brands Hatch. He remembered that he had just won a saloon car race and the satisfaction had been immense; with all the rain after the prolonged dry spell, the circuit had been like a skating rink and he had shown the youngsters, most of them his juniors by at least twenty years, a clean pair of heels. He knew, as they all did, that in rallying and motor racing you need to keep on winning, otherwise the sponsors had a nasty habit of looking elsewhere, and that afternoon he had demonstrated to them all that he hadn't lost the knack.

Craven still didn't remember the start of the journey back — retrograde amnesia they had called it — and he had no idea why he had been driving; Penny usually took the wheel after his races so that he could unwind. Most of the others couldn't understand how he could bear to be driven by anyone else, let alone go off to sleep while they were doing it, but he could and frequently did. Penny had been a safe and accomplished driver and he had every confidence in her, confidence gained over many tens of thousands of miles both in England and on the Continent.

He had been so used to dozing off in the car after race meetings that he must have done just that, but this time he had been behind the wheel and ten minutes after setting out, they had gone off the road and hit a tree. The car was a complete write-off and he recovered consciousness a fortnight later with several square inches of his skull missing. Everybody said he was lucky to be alive, but there wasn't much luck about the reality; he had sustained a depressed fracture of the skull, the bone had become infected and had to be removed and perhaps worst of all, during his period of unconsciousness he had several fits, which effectively ruined his chances of ever going back to competitive driving or for that matter of doing any other form of driving job for a living.

As for Penny, she had not been so badly hurt, but even the skill of the best plastic surgeon in the country failed to disguise the fact that her looks, of which she had been so justly proud, had gone for ever. Apart from the scars on her forehead, the nerve supplying the muscles of one side of her face had been damaged irretrievably so that she was unable to close her left eye properly and every lop-sided movement she made when she spoke or smiled was a constant reminder of what had happened. She was so self conscious about her looks that even a visit to the shops was an ordeal and she refused to eat in public, being so ashamed of her humiliating tendency to dribble. She began to drink and who could blame her, he thought, certainly not him, the one who had been the cause of all her misery and unhappiness.

As far as he was concerned, he realised now that he would have done much better to have accepted the surgeon's offer of putting a metal plate in the defect in his skull. Having that soft, pulsating, sunken area not only made it impossible for him to forget the whole sorry affair, but every prospective employer looked at him as if he were a freak and sapped all his self confidence. He was also in mortal terror of a blow on the head and wore a hat whenever he could, another thing that set him apart from most men of his age. Why, then, had he not let them get on with it? The answer was simple — he had been the cause of Penny's drinking and he must be there to help her. In truth, he realised that a week or two with him out of the way might have done her some good — she seemed both dependent on and resentful of him all at the same time — but she couldn't face her family or former friends and when it came to it, he didn't have the heart to leave her on her own; however imperfect, he was the only person she had.

Previously, Craven had had no idea that anyone could become an alcoholic so quickly. He had known, of course, that she had always liked a drink and God knows, there had always been plenty of people hanging around the hotels in which they used to stay, ready and willing to stand her one, but he had never known her to be the worse for wear, until that is he came out of hospital, by which time she was up to a bottle of spirits a day.

To help her, and also on account of his anti-convulsant drugs, he gave up drinking completely himself and on several occasions had thought that she was cured, but every time, after a few weeks, there came the mounting irritability, followed by sudden periods of good humour and tranquillity, which had only one possible explanation. He had become an expert in finding hidden bottles, for God's sake.

★ ★ ★

Craven didn't know whether it was just the effects of an eighteen hour break from the anti-convulsant drugs or the events of the previous evening that had worked the trick, but for whatever reason, there was no doubt that when he woke the following morning, he felt better than he had done since the accident.

In the cold light of day, though, he was appalled by the risks he had taken. The neurologist at the rehabilitation centre had been at great pains to point out that head injuries had a cumulative effect and that at all costs he must avoid any direct blow to the area of the bony defect. He had not been so carried away by his victory over the massive thug that he believed that it had been due to anything other than a piece of the greatest good luck and one solid blow from that enormous fist of his would undoubtedly have reduced him to a cabbage.

Craven went round to the Abbey Nursing Home after lunch and wished later that he hadn't.

'If you'd telephoned me first,' McAlister said in his usual abrupt manner when Craven arrived, 'it would have saved you a journey. We don't often see it these days, but when she came round this morning, your wife was suffering from acute alcoholic hallucinosis.'

'The D.T.s, you mean.'

'Not exactly, though it is similar in some ways. She is getting persecutory, aural hallucinations and unfortunately most of them are centred on you; the voices are telling her that you disfigured her and that you are being unfaithful to her. At the moment, if you see her I fear she might try to attack you.'

'How long will it take her to recover?'

'Two or three weeks at least, I'm afraid, and that'll only be for the acute episode.' He put his arm round Craven's shoulders. 'Don't worry, I should be able to get her moved some time next week and she'll be in good hands with Dobson.'

'But what about the future?'

'I think you may have to resign yourself to the fact that she will have to be in hospital for several months.'

Privately, McAlister didn't think she stood much chance of ever getting out — the woman just seemed to have no will to give up drinking and precious little to live. One of these days, he thought, she would probably commit suicide and he couldn't help thinking that that would probably be the best solution for the poor woman and her wretched husband. He had seldom felt so utterly defeated by a case; if half the things she had told him were true, then Craven was a monster, but apart from the fact that the man had always seemed perfectly reasonable to him, trying to sort out fact from fantasy and both of them from her delusions was a well nigh impossible task. One thing, though, was crystal clear and that was that she hated her husband with a deep loathing and in her present state she was a positive danger to him.

★　★　★

Craven was even more certain that the drugs had been quietly poisoning him when on the following morning he even managed to find both the energy and concentration to start the daunting task of trying to put his financial affairs into some kind of order. It was when he was sorting out some bills that he had stuffed casually into his jacket pocket some days before that he came across the card that the woman had given him. He hadn't even read the name on it before; Claire Markham — he liked the name Claire and somehow it suited her to perfection.

As Craven thought about her, all the curiosity he had so assiduously repressed, came to the surface and he sat back, trying to picture her in his mind. When he really tried, he was surprised to find how clear an impression he had of her. She must have been in her late twenties, tallish for a woman — even with her modest heels, she was much the same height as him — and he would have said elegant rather than beautiful. Perhaps her most striking feature was the colour of her dark eyes, which almost seemed to match her lovely, raven-black hair, the sort that actually glistened in the light, and the over-all impression of calm serenity was underlined by the quiet and tasteful way she had been dressed.

She was tough — the big man had not been fooling about when he had hit her and yet within minutes she seemed to have been able to ignore it; she was perceptive — she had noticed his head at once and yet had obviously divined how sensitive he was to it — and his physical reaction to his thoughts about her, made it abundantly clear how attractive he had found her. He suddenly realised with a sense of shock that he had not even so much as thought of a woman in that way since the accident and all his anxieties in that direction came suddenly to the surface. Along with so many other things, he had thought that that side of his life was over for ever and knew instinctively that it would take time to come to terms with the fact that it obviously wasn't.

To help to take his mind off the subject, he started to speculate about the possible motives there might have been for the men wanting to attack her. It could hardly have been robbery — they could have snatched her handbag and the single strand of pearls from around her neck in a second. Rape? He didn't think so — the place was wrong and so was the method of attack. There was only one way to find out; he put on his best suit, gave his shoes a special shine and looked at the card once again. Whatever else came out of it, he had an instinct that he would get a good lunch and that would be an unusual enough experience for him in all conscience.

The window of the restaurant was full of flowers, unusually, there was no tariff on view outside and on the door was the simple legend 'MARKHAM'S' with underneath in small print: 'Advance Reservations Only'. Craven hesitated for a moment outside, then opened the door and walked in.

'Good afternoon, sir. Did you wish to make a reservation?'

The strikingly pretty girl, wearing a black dress and a white apron with lace edges, smiled at him and offered him a card.

'No, thank you. Claire Markham asked me to lunch a short time ago, but I should have warned her that I was coming today.' He looked round the room, which was obviously full. 'I can see that you're very busy, perhaps it would be better if I tried on another day.'

'That's all right, sir, I'll let her know you're here. What name is it?'

'Craven. Michael Craven.'

The girl came back within a minute or two and once again gave him a flashing smile. 'Mrs. Markham was expecting you; she's busy just at the moment, but said she'd join you as soon as she possibly could. If you'd like to take a seat, I'll clear this table for you.'

Craven had felt a momentary stab of disappointment at the Mrs. — typically, he thought, he hadn't noticed whether or not she had been wearing a wedding ring when he had seen her before — but gave her full marks for thought reading, or perhaps it would have been more appropriate to call it clairvoyance. He would never have come if he hadn't come across the card by accident — or would he? Already, he could feel his excitement growing at the prospect of seeing her again.

In fact, although she did appear briefly to welcome him, he didn't have a chance to speak to her properly until after three o'clock. During the time he was waiting for her, he had a leisurely lunch, which was quite excellent, and also had ample opportunity to observe how the place was run. At first sight it was difficult to understand how it could possibly be making any money — there were only enough places for about forty people and the menu was extremely limited for such an expensive restaurant — but after a time, he began to get the hang of the formula.

In the first place, all the tables had been reserved and were full — he had been given one normally used for stacking plates — secondly, there were just two sittings for lunch and finally, the three girls who were doing the serving were attractive, good humoured, knowledgeable and seemed, and he was quite sure were, genuinely pleased to see the patrons. The cooking, the choice of food and the wines were all first class, the service was impeccable and there were obviously quite enough people who found that combination more than compensated for the restricted choice.

Craven had no means of knowing how much of the actual cooking Claire had done, but she had certainly been on her feet and in and out of the kitchen for the whole of the couple of hours that he had been in the restaurant and yet, when she came across to him when the last people had gone, she still contrived to look just as cool and elegant as she had been when he had met her before.

'Enjoy your lunch?'

'Immensely, thanks.'

'Good. I usually take a shower and have a couple of hours relaxation in my flat at this time of day; care to come along? I think perhaps that after the other night I need a protector and in any case, I owe you an explanation.'

She didn't say anything further either then or during the short walk to her flat, which was considerable relief to Craven, who felt both tongue-tied and dry mouthed, yet another indication, if that were needed, how much he had been disturbed by her. To his shame, he was half expecting her to appear after her shower in a seductive négligé and take him off to her bedroom as a final demonstration of her thanks; when she did come in, dressed in a crisp white blouse and blue skirt, to his profound embarrassment he felt himself beginning to blush and to hide it, he took out his handkerchief and made a great show of stifling a sneeze.

'It must be hard work running that restaurant.'

'It is. It cost me a great deal of time and effort to build it up and I've no intention of letting it go now. I've no right to involve a complete stranger in my problems, but it would help me a great deal to talk about it — that's why I'm so glad you've come.' She gave him a smile that immediately provoked violent palpitations that were almost painful in their intensity. 'My husband Bob was a surgeon and two years after we were married, he was found to have Hodgkin's disease and three years after that, he was dead.' She intercepted Craven's look towards the photograph on the desk. 'Yes, that's right, that's him — I suppose he would have been about your age when he died.

'There must be any number of ways of trying to come to terms with a situation like that, but the one I chose was hard work. Bob had been very well insured and I sank most of the money into the restaurant. Why did I choose that particular line of business? Well, there were two reasons; in the first place that type of thing runs in the family — my father still runs an hotel in Torquay — and secondly it helped to remind me of some of the good times I had with Bob. He always used to get such pleasure out of eating well and wine testing was a hobby of his.

'My preparations were helped enormously and a lot of the stimulus came from my friendship with Maurice Bellancourt, who is a restaurateur in Paris. Bob was an accident surgeon and he operated on Maurice's son when he was involved in a road accident while on holiday in this country. As a thank-you present he invited us both over to spend the weekend with him in Paris and that's how our friendship developed.

'I've always tried to bear in mind what Maurice said to me right at the outset: 'in the restaurant business, to be good you have to be expensive, but being expensive doesn't make you good.' He has helped me in so many different ways; he sent me a chef who needed experience on his own, he advised me to make an arrangement with a good wine importer and finally he convinced me of the value of first class service.

'Of course what we have to offer doesn't suit everybody; we will only accept people who have a reservation, the menu, as you saw, is very restricted for choice and we only open five days a week. I ran it at a loss for about a year, but now it's doing very well. I have managed to build up a regular clientele, the place has now developed a certain reputation for quality, particularly after it was favourably reviewed in one of the Sunday papers, and the fact that it is both select and rather expensive makes it desirable for some people.'

'Do you do some of the cooking yourself?'

'Yes, a little.'

'I thought so. That apple pie was absolutely delicious and it could never have been cooked by a Frenchman.'

Craven saw at once from the slight flush that came up on her cheeks that he had said the right thing.

'It was obvious to me that it would be no earthly good trying to compete with Georges — he's in a different class from me — but I like to think that some of the things I do, largely traditional English dishes, are complementary to his efforts and I rather specialise in sweets.'

'I can see how proud you must be of the whole concern. How about Georges? Has he been with you from the start?'

She gave a laugh. 'I don't think that Maurice is all that pleased about him; he has become such an anglophile that I don't think he has the slightest intention of going back. Eventually I think he would really like to start a place of his own.'

'And the girls? I was very impressed by them.'

'I have an arrangement with the head of a catering school and I take two or three of their students for a couple of months at a time. Inevitably their quality varies a bit — the ones we have at the moment are excellent — but on the whole they are hard working, enthusiastic and pleasant and you can't ask for more than that.'

'And now, I suppose, someone is trying to run you out of business.'

'You're not far off the mark. A little over four weeks ago, someone rang up to say that unless I paid them £100 a week, unpleasant things would start to happen to me, that I was not to go to the police and they would get in touch with me later on about the method of payment.'

'What did you do?'

'I went straight to the police, of course. The inspector who interviewed me couldn't have been nicer, but they weren't able to achieve anything very useful apart from putting a tap on my phone in case I was rung up again. They kept it up for a couple of weeks and then, when nothing had happened, decided that it was probably nothing but a practical joke; I must say that I was inclined to agree with them until the other night.'

'What exactly happened?'

'I always walk home along the same route and have never had any trouble before, but that night I noticed those two men following me and started to run, hoping to find a policeman. They caught up with me in that passage-way and the rest you know. Incidentally, what on earth did you do to that man?'

'I just boxed his ears fairly enthusiastically. I don't know what the medical explanation is, but a friend of mine told me once that it could cause sudden loss of consciousness.'

'I should think you probably ruptured both his ear drums.'

'What do you propose to do now?'

'I've been trying to decide ever since it

happened. I rang the police again directly after you had left and told them what had happened; I don't think they really believed me until I showed them this when they came round.' She pulled up her blouse and gently touched the purple bruise which was discolouring her white skin. 'I somehow didn't think you'd want to get involved, so that's why I waited until you had gone. I just said that some strange man had rescued me in the nick of time, but I told them I was too distraught at the time to recollect any useful details of what you looked like.' She intercepted his smile. 'What's so funny?'

'The idea that you might ever get distraught.'

She gave him a long look with her very steady, dark eyes. 'You don't know me.'

Once, Craven would have known precisely what she meant by that remark, but that was a long time ago; not only was he hopelessly out of practice where women were concerned, but he just wasn't ready for any involvement, physical or emotional, with anyone. He realised that he ought to tell Claire about himself and Penny, but he didn't know how to begin and then the opportunity was lost as she got up to get them a cup of tea.

All the time she was out of the room, Craven was dreading her return, breaking out in a cold sweat at the thought of failure if her remark really meant what he thought it did. When she did come back with the tray, though, she behaved so naturally that he almost managed to convince himself that he had imagined both what she had said and the look that went with it.

She poured out the tea, frowning slightly with concentration, and then paused with her cup half way to her mouth.

'I don't know whether their object is to milk me of all the money they can, or whether they aim to close my business down completely, but either way it seems to me that I've only got three choices; I can pay up, get out, or fight them. As I've no intention of letting whoever they are get away with it, you've no doubt guessed what the answer's going to be.'

'But why should they have singled you out?'

'I would imagine it's because I'm the smallest and weakest link in the catering chain around here. I suppose their thinking might be that if I refused to pay or went to the police and they then made an example of me 'pour encourager les autres', no doubt the others would be more likely to cooperate.'

'Have any of the others been approached?'

'Not so far as I know; certainly, according to the Inspector, no one else has complained to them, but then that might not mean all that much — some of my colleagues aren't over-enamoured of the police.'

'And I suppose as the other night's exhibition failed to succeed, you're afraid that they might try something else.'

'Precisely. And I'm pretty vulnerable, you know. They've only got to throw a fire-bomb through the window, get at Georges, or put me out of commission in some way and that'll be that. As far as the police are concerned, I don't see what they can do if these people are in no hurry — there's obviously a limit both to the length of time they can give me protection and the efficiency with which they can keep it up.'

'Are they keeping an eye on you at the moment?'

'Yes. They've stationed a man outside the restaurant and they also suggested that I made sure that I was accompanied whenever I went out.'

'What about this flat?'

'Well, as you saw, there is a porter on duty throughout the twenty-four hours and the lock and chain on the door are pretty solid.'

'I wouldn't have thought that that was all that impressive; I'm not doing anything for the next week or two, so if I can be of any help . . . '

My God, he thought, as soon as he'd said it, what have I let myself in for? Then, almost in the same moment, he realised that he meant it.

Claire looked at him for a long time before replying. 'What exactly had you in mind?'

'Well, I was thinking that someone

ought to be looking after you and if they contact you again, you could pretend to be frightened of them, pay up the first instalment and when they collect it, we could try to find out who they are by helping the police to set a trap.'

She came across and kissed him on the forehead. 'You're a strange man, Michael Craven. You rescue me from that great ogre, you offer to help me further and I still don't know the first thing about you.'

Craven was not a vain man and knew perfectly well that his anonymity was all part of the game and the thing that excited her most about him and so he merely smiled and looked away.

'I have no right to involve you in all this, but if you really mean it, it would make things very much easier for me; Georges has been seeing me home, but it's not fair to ask him to keep it up — not only has he got his own life to lead, but this type of thing's not his scene at all; he's scared stiff of the whole business, although he'd never admit it. You could stay here, if you like — it might save you a lot of trouble.'

Claire realised at once how badly she had put it and found herself blushing when Craven accepted, being glad to be left to herself when he went off a few minutes later to collect some clothes from his flat. She stood at the window watching him walk along the street and wondering why on earth she had asked a man in his forties, about whom she knew nothing apart from the fact that he had obviously had a major operation on his head, to stay in her flat. She had in fact done it entirely on the spur of the moment, but even at this stage didn't regret it one bit, which was perhaps the most extraordinary thing of all.

3

No doubt a judge in a divorce court would never have believed it, but that night and the two following, Craven slept in the spare room and Claire tried, none too successfully, to do the same in the large double bed in the adjoining one. Normally a good sleeper, each night she spent hours trying to drop off and with every squeaking board was half afraid that he was going to come into her room and then almost cried with frustration and disappointment when he didn't.

If only she had been secure in that side of her life with her husband Bob, she would have known what to do, but she hadn't and she didn't. Since Bob's death she had had very little contact with men apart from Georges, who didn't really count, and the one other incident, which although it had been unpleasant at the time, she had succeeded in putting right out of her mind straight away. Now, though, she was discovering things about herself that she had hardly even suspected and she was more than a little ashamed of some of them.

To Craven, those two days were also in some ways an anticlimax; no one tried to contact Claire, he was certain that they weren't followed either to or from the flat and the restaurant remained busy and crowded. In other ways, though, they were a sheer delight; he helped to show people to their seats, made the bookings, picked up the rudiments of waiting and basked in the glow of feeling fit and alert for the first time since the accident.

If anyone had told him twenty years earlier that he would have been able to spend three nights alone in the same flat as an attractive woman without finishing up in her bed, he would never have believed them, but now, after that first evening, it seemed quite natural to him. He told himself that he couldn't possibly take advantage of someone like Claire, who was after all nearly twenty years younger than him, just because her judgement had been affected by the strain she was going through, but deep down he knew it was just an excuse and the real reason was that he was terrified of making a fool of himself. In fact, since the accident, he had only tried a couple of times with Penny and both of them had been an unmitigated disaster.

The one fly in the ointment as far as he was concerned was Georges. The man was just too good looking, Craven thought, too sure of his own attraction and the looks he gave Claire when he thought no one was watching, could have had only one interpretation. Once or twice too, Craven had seen him lean over her to inspect some dish she was cooking and there was no doubt what he was up to then either. To make matters worse as far as he was concerned, once, when he was watching them through the half-open door of the kitchen, he saw that she had her arm round his shoulders and was speaking to him with an intensity that suggested a relationship much deeper than mere employer and employee. The fact that he knew perfectly well that he had no proprietary rights to her and was just being stupidly jealous didn't help at all.

On the Friday evening of that first week, Craven was just showing some people out, when an Indian in a fawn suit came hurrying in and asked for Claire. It was obvious that he was in a high state of agitation and he spoke to her for a good five minutes with a wealth of gesture. From time to time, when the pitch of the man's voice rose high in agitation, Craven was just able to catch some of his words.

'Absolutely impossible . . . ruination . . . Kiren and the boys.'

When eventually he finished, Craven could see Claire talking to him earnestly, holding his hand in hers and she clearly managed to calm him down, as by the time she showed him to the door, he was nodding his head briskly and thanking her profusely.

'What was all that about?'

'That was Meswani. He runs an Indian restaurant just up the road and they've threatened to harm his children unless he pays up. Things are difficult enough for him anyway — his wife died a couple of years ago and his fifteen year old daughter looks after things for him at home, including the care of the two small boys. I feel very sorry for the girl; I don't consider it fair to expect an adolescent of that age to have all the responsibility of a family, but Meswani doesn't see it in that light at all. He takes a typically Indian view of the place of women in society and doesn't seem to appreciate that the wretched Kiren is bound to compare her lot with that of her English contemporaries, most of whom don't do a hand's turn at home and go out regularly with boyfriends. Anyway, Meswani dotes on his children and as he's in a chronic state of agitation at the best of times, you can imagine what this has done to him.'

'What did you say?'

'We both belong to a small association of restaurant owners and I suggested that he went round to as many of the other members as he could and found out if anyone else had been threatened and then we can plan what to do.'

'I suppose it's some consolation that

there is someone else in the same boat.'

'Yes. That's exactly what I told Meswani and I also suggested that he asked Signor Morruzzi, the chairman of our association, to call a meeting. Perhaps I shouldn't say this, but some of the members aren't all that reputable and they keep their ears fairly close to the Soho ground; that means that there is a good chance that one of them will have heard something. I'm hoping that the meeting will be organised for tomorrow. Would you be good enough to come along with me? Up to now, my methods of dealing with the problem don't seem to have been a wild success and I could do with a bit of moral support.'

'I'd be glad to.'

★   ★   ★

The meeting was held in one of the private dining rooms on the second floor of Enrico Morruzzi's restaurant at ten o'clock on the Saturday morning. Apart from Werner Maier, who ran a bierkeller, they were the first to arrive and after

Claire had introduced him, they sat down and she whispered the names of the others as they filed in. Altogether there were about twenty people present and they were a motley collection. Looking round, Craven realised that he and Claire were the only English people present; he still didn't feel sure enough of his relationship with her to make any comment, but nevertheless couldn't help wondering what she was doing involving herself with what looked to him like the riff-raff of the Eastern end of the Mediterranean basin.

There was an expectant hush as the stocky, elderly man with a shock of iron-grey hair came into the room, accompanied by a rather small, but very good looking young man. The Italian sat down at the head of the table and held up his hand for silence.

'Before we start the formal business,' he said in his slow, heavily accented English, 'I must ask your friend to leave, Mrs. Markham. It is one of the rules of our association that only the owners are present at our discussions.'

Craven started to get to his feet, but Claire put a restraining hand on his arm.

'I know of no such rule, Signor Morruzzi and if it does exist, may I ask in that case what your nephew is doing here? Mr. Craven is my partner and if you insist on him leaving, then I will go too.'

'I was not aware that you had a partner, Mrs. Markham.' He nodded in Craven's direction and although his measured way of speaking didn't alter, it was obvious that beneath his correct exterior, he was seething. 'Lady and gentlemen,' he continued, 'I understand that several of our number here today, including myself, have received various demands for protection money and the purpose of this meeting is to decide what course of action we should take. I for one will not tolerate such a thing — they have had the temerity to threaten to destroy my wine cellar in the country unless I pay.' He raised both hands in a gesture that said more than any words could have done. 'If anyone so much as tries, I will crush them.'

'That's all very well for you, but I am

on my own. How am I going to guard my property?'

'I think we should pay — my children.'

'We should go to the police.'

Everyone began to speak at once and Craven was quite convinced that absolutely nothing was going to be achieved until Claire suddenly stood up. He could see from the tightening of Morruzzi's lips that the Italian didn't like the interruption and he motioned her to sit down, but although it was obvious that Claire was nervous, there was no hint of a tremor in her voice and she did not drop her eyes.

'As the only person here who has actually suffered a physical assault — and if it hadn't been for Mr. Craven here, it would have been a very serious one — I think I have a clear right to voice my opinion.'

'Hear, hear!' Craven said loudly and looked back aggressively at the several stares that came his way.

'Let us give her a courteous hearing.'

'Thank you, Herr Maier. The first thing I would say is that we must all stick together and trust the police to help us. I have already reported everything that has happened to me and if only we all do the same, surely these people will be caught quickly. If we pay up, try to protect ourselves individually, or simply do nothing, all we'll achieve is to play straight into their hands. Most of you here have larger businesses than mine, some with branches in other parts of the country, and are big enough and strong enough to cope on your own, but I am not; I have just the one small restaurant and if that is put out of action in any way, I will be finished. I propose that we ask a representative of the Metropolitan Police to meet us here as soon as possible.'

Claire sat down and after a moment's silence, Craven began to applaud. To his considerable embarrassment, no one but the German, Maier, joined in and he very soon stopped. It very quickly became even clearer just how little support Claire had; some of those present didn't even appear to believe that she had been assaulted at all and that she was making the whole thing up, while others, like Morruzzi, hinted darkly that they knew who was behind it and that they were perfectly capable of dealing with the threat themselves without the need for any interference from the police.

The meeting broke up after nearly an hour without anything constructive having been decided and with obvious reluctance, Claire agreed with the majority view that the police should be left out of it for the time being.

'Sooner or later,' Morruzzi said, 'they will send someone to collect the money; you all have my telephone number and I guarantee to send help at any time of the day or night and within a matter of minutes.'

'But that won't be any good to me if they throw a fire bomb into my premises.'

'If you had come to me in the first place, you would not have had to endure that unpleasant assault, my dear young lady,' he replied smoothly. 'Wasn't it you yourself who said that we should all stick together? I have men working for me who know this area like the backs of their hands and they are a better insurance policy than your police. Give my nephew a detailed description of the men who tried to beat you up and they will be found — mark my words.'

'At least let us agree to meet again if anyone else receives threats or any other information comes to light.'

'I was just about to suggest the same thing myself.' The Italian rose to his feet and bowing slightly towards the others, walked slowly out of the room.

Craven hadn't liked the look of Morruzzi's nephew, Carlo, from the moment he set eyes on him and further acquaintance did nothing to make him change his mind. He hadn't been around the racing circuits of the world for more than twenty years without knowing his sort well. He had been watching the young Italian while Claire had been speaking and even though Craven accepted that pure, unadulterated lust was a difficult emotion to hide, Carlo had made a notably poor job of doing it.

Claire didn't appear to have noticed anything and Craven at least had sufficient insight to realise that he was a fine one to talk. He watched her as she frowned slightly, concentrating on giving a description of the two men who attacked her; the truth of the matter was that he was jealous of Carlo, jealous both of his youth and his good looks. He was immediately ashamed of himself and made an attempt at concentrating on what she was saying.

'He was tall — about six foot two or three — very large and battered looking, with a broken nose, cauliflower ears and close-cropped sandy hair.'

'What about the other one?'

'I didn't really see him — he was behind me for most of the time.'

Carlo didn't actually smile, but Craven could have sworn that he was finding the whole thing amusing and had an almost irresistible desire to hit him.

'And what about you, my friend? Have you any details to add?'

'If your sources of information are anything like as good as your uncle claims, then you should have no difficulty in picking up the big fellow — by the look of him, he's spent a good deal of time in fair-ground boxing booths. As to the other, he was very small — a bit bigger than you, I'd say, but without quite your looks; in fact he had a passing resemblance to a ferret, with a straggling brown moustache and shifty eyes.'

Claire marvelled, not for the first time, how childish men could be, but at the same time thought that if she allowed it to go on much longer, they would be at each other's throats.

'Do those descriptions mean anything to you, Carlo?'

The man did not appear to have heard the question, getting up and striding out of the room without saying another word, an angry flush on his cheeks.

'Who does that miserable little pimp think he is?' Craven said as they left the restaurant and started to make their way back to the flat.

'Go easy with him, Mike. He's only a boy really and there was no need to antagonise him like that; if we get across Morruzzi it'll only make things more difficult. I admit I got carried away a bit at the meeting myself, but it's no good us preaching the virtues of sticking together if we stir things up ourselves.'

'Perhaps you're right,' he said grudgingly. 'I reckon, though, that several of those business friends of yours are on the fiddle or something.'

'Mike, that's just prejudice; what on earth makes you say that? They've all been most kind and welcoming to me — that's one of the reasons why I accepted their invitation to join the group.'

'No, it isn't. It stands to reason; just look at the way they reacted to your suggestion about calling in the police.'

Claire thought for a moment before replying. 'I was so tense and worked up at the time that I didn't think about it, but I see what you mean. You must remember, though, that many foreigners and immigrants take a very different view of the police from us and fear of them might be the reason why they don't want to get involved. Talking of immigrants, though, it wouldn't surprise me if some of the employees of the Cypriots and Indians were here illegally, which may be another explanation.'

'How about Morruzzi? He's a 'Godfather' figure if ever I saw one.'

Claire laughed. 'He's a bit pompous all right, but he's not a bad sort really and he's been very helpful to me, particularly with the wines. In fact, that's how the association came to be formed; he supplies us all. He's a big importer and has got a place in the country with a vast cellar — I went to a tasting there once. He also runs a chain of clubs and restaurants. The one we've just left is the biggest and best; some of the others are not quite so respectable either — you know the sort of thing, topless bars and the like.'

'There you are, you see; I knew there was something fishy about him.'

'Mike, you're nothing but an old puritan.'

Craven shrugged his shoulders, 'What's next on the agenda?'

'Well, I don't know about you, but I've had just about enough of all this for the time being. Why don't we go out into the country somewhere and forget all about it? I know it's still early in the year, but it's a lovely day and quite warm enough to eat outside.'

'Good idea.'

They prepared a picnic lunch together and when they went down to the basement garage where she kept her Mini Cooper, Claire tossed the keys over to him. Craven was within an ace of succumbing to the temptation; he had had some very successful seasons in saloon car racing and rally-cross and Minis had always suited his style. He fielded the bunch neatly and then handed them back with deep regret.

'It's nice of you to offer, but I don't drive.'

Most women, Craven thought, would have questioned him or at least made a comment, but not Claire; she merely nodded, picked up the picnic basket and climbed in to the car, giving him a smile as he fastened the seat belt on the passenger side.

'All set? Right, let's go, shall we?'

★ ★ ★

The place he had selected for their picnic had been an airfield during the war and soon after, a friend of his had bought and farmed it for a while. When that had proved a failure, he had started a water skiing club at the nearby lake and now he had plans to open a country club, but it was obvious that nothing much was coming out of that idea. Craven hadn't been there for a couple of years and was half expecting to find building work going on, but the place was utterly deserted.

They had only just had time to lay out the rug some fifty yards from the lake-side, when the men came out of the shelter of the small copse and sprinted towards them through the heather. This time there were three of them. Craven recognised the one who had held Claire in the alley-way at once, but the leader seemed to be the thick-set man who was carrying the sawn-off shotgun.

Perhaps the most terrifying aspect of the whole thing was that for several minutes none of them said a single word. The man with the gun motioned Craven towards the Mini and his finger tightened on the trigger when he hesitated and looked round. It was a futile gesture, in any case, as the man gave him no chance either of getting away or of grabbing the gun, keeping his distance the whole way there, but never being far enough away to make a dash for safety a practical proposition.

'Get in the passenger seat and do up the safety belt.'

The man stood there pointing the gun through the open window, while the other two frog-marched Claire along until she was standing ten paces directly in front of the car.

'Let her go,' Craven shouted.

The two men released her arms and withdrew a few feet, but never once took their eyes off her.

'Strip!'

Craven saw her hesitate and look round with a haunted expression on her face.

'If you don't do exactly what I say, I'm going to put my thumb over that place on your boy friend's head and press — it will be quite interesting to see what happens.'

Claire put her fingers on the top button

of her blouse and quickly took all her clothes off, standing there, staring directly ahead, her head held erect and with her back as straight as a ram-rod. One of the two men behind her laughed coarsely, but apart from a slight tightening of her jaw, she failed to react at all.

'The boss warned you what would happen if you went to the police — this time you won't get away with it as easily as you did the other night.'

The man standing by the car then proceeded to tell her in all its obscene detail precisely what they proposed to do to her. When he had finished, he nodded and while one of the other two put an arm lock on her, the other raised his hand. The sound of the first vicious blow rang out like a pistol shot and Claire's head jerked to one side, an angry looking flush spreading over her bruised cheek. As the man got ready to hit her again, Craven shut his eyes and ground his teeth together in despair.

'Open your eyes and watch it — watch all of it.'

He reached in through the window and

started to force Craven's eyes open, thrusting his head so close that he could feel his breath on his cheek. At the same instant that he heard the sound of the second blow from outside, he reached up with his right hand, grasped a fistful of the man's hair and pulled down as hard as he could.

A racing driver's hands and arms get very strong and although the man tried to jerk his head free, he never had a chance. He let out a high-pitched scream of agony and his hands went up to reach for the fingers that were torturing his scalp, but before he could reach them, Craven started to wind up the window with his left hand. The man tried desperately to prevent it from ascending, gripping the upper edge with his fingers, but already it was under his chin and his head was trapped.

He made one last effort to pull the glass down, but Craven released his hair and with one quick movement bent back the man's left little finger until it broke with a dry snapping sound, as easily as if it had been a piece of chalk. The man let out another shriek of pain, his hands disappeared and giving the window handle a last turn, Craven locked the door, unfastened the safety belt and within seconds was behind the wheel.

The man who had hit Claire was staring at them over his shoulder with an expression of horror on his face, but when the engine started up, began to run towards the car.

'Tell them both to clear off and make it snappy, or I'll let out the clutch and break your neck.'

Craven revved up the engine and the man began to shout out as loudly as the pressure under his chin would allow.

'Les! Let her go! For God's sake . . . '

His voice rose to a howl as the car moved forward a couple of yards and he frantically tried to keep to his feet. The man approaching stopped in mid-stride, the one holding Claire let go of her arm and then they both began to back away and fled into the trees and out of sight.

'Claire, are you O.K.?'

There were two angry blotches on her left cheek and a cut at the angle of her jaw where the man's signet ring had caught her, but her voice was quite steady when she replied.

'I'm fine, thanks.'

'That's the spirit. Get dressed then, will you, then sling the gun into the back of the car and I'll have a little chat with our friend here.'

He kept the Mini going quite slowly in a circle on the grass and the man made every effort to keep his feet, but after only a short distance he stumbled and for a moment Craven thought he had strangled himself, but then he began to recover his breath as the car came to a halt.

'All right, my friend, let's have it all. Who's behind this and why are they doing it?'

To give emphasis to what he had said, he blipped the accelerator and the man let out a bellow of fear.

'I don't know,' he shouted.

'What do you mean, you don't know? Pull the other one.'

The car leaped forward a further yard and the man's face went purple and this time a good two minutes went by before he was able to speak again.

'It's true, I swear it. I get the instructions over the phone and even when I'm paid, I never see the bloke.'

'How do they hand over the money?'

'I'm given the number of a hotel bedroom and a time and the money's always waiting inside.'

'You're very trusting, I must say.'

'We've worked for the same bloke a number of times and he's always played fair.'

'I see. And what instructions did you receive this time?'

'On the first occasion we were just to beat her up a bit — not too badly, just enough to teach her a lesson.'

'What about the second?'

'He told us to make a better job of it — really smash her face in and make you watch.'

'Oh he did, did he? And when exactly did you get these last instructions?'

'A couple of days after we'd tried the first time.'

'How did he know you'd failed?'

'Search me. He did say that this time

he wouldn't pay us until he'd seen the results.'

'How did you find us here so easily?'

'We were watching her flat and followed you out of London.'

'You said you were just told to beat her up. What about the other things you were threatening?'

'That was just to give the boys a bit of fun.'

Craven let out the clutch with a bang, dragging the man forwards a few yards and when he stopped thought for a terrible moment that he'd overdone it and killed him. After a minute or two, though, he began to breathe again and Craven wound down the window, gave his face a push and watched while the man lay on the grass, wheezing and groaning.

Claire had just got into the car, when in the rear-view mirror, Craven saw the gun-metal grey Ford bucketing across the grass towards them. He could only think that the man behind the wheel rather fancied his ability to corner them or run them off into the trees, but he never had a chance. Craven had cut his teeth on auto-cross courses much rougher than the terrain surrounding them, special stages of rallies were second nature to him and a brief smile passed over his face.

'Do your belt up as tightly as you can,' he shouted at Claire, then settled himself comfortably, the front wheels spinning madly as he lifted his foot off the clutch.

The long lay-off might have made a difference in a competition, but not with the indifferent opposition facing him. Within seconds he was completely at home; if he had really tried, he could have lost them inside five minutes, but the opportunity was too good to miss and for the next quarter of an hour he enjoyed himself hugely. At times on the concrete surface of the runway, at times on the grass and at times on the sandy area near the trees, he led them a merry dance, neither leaving them so far behind that they became discouraged, nor allowing them too close for his own comfort.

Being able to read the terrain and having an eye for different types of surface are absolute essentials for rally and auto-cross drivers and Craven had always had that ability to a very high degree. However careful a reconnaissance was carried out — and there had been no one on the circuit more obsessional about that than him — the unexpected was always cropping up and one of his advantages had been the ability to react much more quickly than most of the opposition. On this occasion, though, there was plenty of time to select the exact spot with care and when he tired of the sport, he let them close to within thirty feet. Just short of a soft, sandy area, he spun the wheel and at exactly the right moment, turned the power on; the Mini's front wheels bit into the turf and they made the turn with six feet to spare.

As he had hoped and expected, the driver of the Escort over-shot slightly and half way round the turn, with the car broadside on, the off side wheels sank into the soft sand. Looking back, Craven saw the Ford heel over, make two complete somersaults and finish up back on its wheels, its roof hideously dented.

Craven drove slowly back to the clearing by the lake to collect the rug and the picnic basket. The man was still sitting on the ground massaging his neck, but at their approach, got shakily to his feet and tried to run away. His legs weren't up to it; his knees buckled and he measured his length on the ground.

Craven took the shotgun off the back seat and got out of the car, standing six feet short of the man in case he was shamming.

'Take off your jacket and trousers.' When the man hesitated, he lifted the gun by its barrel and raised it in the air. 'Suit yourself; if you want a tap on the head with this, I'd be only too happy to oblige.'

It was too much to hope that a professional heavy would have any means of identification on him, but there was a thick bundle of notes in his jacket pocket, a flick knife, which Craven sent spinning far out into the lake and an indescribably dirty handkerchief, which he left strictly alone. When he had finished searching them, Craven threw the garments on to the ground.

'Now clear off, my friend, and if I see or hear of you again, I'll spread you half across London. Your car's through those trees and if your luck's in, the others will be alive and that heap still driveable; if not, you'll just have to walk.'

As Craven watched the man dress, drag himself to his feet and limp across the grass, he was still not suffering from the delusion that he was Superman. It was true that he didn't feel quite so shaky as he had on that first occasion, but he was perfectly well aware that once again he had been lucky and he could hardly expect it to go on like this indefinitely. He would have liked nothing more than to have settled down at the lake-side, eaten their picnic lunch and spent the after-noon swimming and lying in the sun, but the men were their only lead and he had no intention of losing them.

He picked up the hamper and the rug, heaved the shotgun into the water and walked slowly back to the Mini. He could hardly accuse Claire of being slow on the uptake, he thought; she was already in the driving seat and gave him a smile as he came up to the window.

'I reckoned that you'd probably want to

follow them and I just remembered that you can't drive.'

Mike Craven managed to stop his teeth chattering long enough to raise what was intended as an answering smile, but the attempt was not a great success.

'I never said that I couldn't drive, just that I didn't.'

'If I could drive half as well as you don't, I wouldn't complain, if you see what I mean. It makes me nervous just sitting here.'

'You drive very well.'

From the shelter of the trees they watched the men trying to prise the buckled near-side wing of the Ford free from the tyre. It was obvious that none of them had been badly hurt in the crash and eventually, after much cursing and swearing, they succeeded in getting the hideously dented vehicle going, driving it slowly back towards the main road.

'Surely they won't go all the way back to London like that.'

'No. My guess is that they'll steal another car — probably of the same make — at the earliest possible opportunity.'

'Go on — it's not as easy as all that, is it?'

'With any luck they'll give you a demonstration and then you'll see.'

Craven reckoned it must have been one of those days when he was psychic; just outside the nearest town, they parked the battered Ford in a lay-by and while he followed them on foot, Claire drove behind in the Mini. The men walked into the large free car park and were away so quickly in another Escort that he had to sprint back to the Mini to enable them to keep it in sight.

'I don't think much of that for a demonstration — they must have had that second car there all along.'

'Don't you believe it; it's possible to open any popular model like that Escort with only half a dozen keys and with a bit of judicious filing, you can reduce it to two or three. Haven't you ever seen the police at it? They can clear a streetful of cars in no time flat if they're really trying. Anyway, one of them had a small bunch of keys; I saw it all quite clearly and he made it at the second attempt.'

'The things I learn when I'm with you!'

Craven glanced sideways at her; the experience that Claire had been through that afternoon would have been enough to put most people in need of sleep treatment for a fortnight, but he could have sworn, that just like the first time, she wasn't in the least scared, merely slightly flushed with excitement.

Being early on a Sunday afternoon, there was very little traffic about and their problem was not that of losing the Ford, but of being seen. The men ahead, though, were not taking any risks of being stopped by the police and kept to all the speed limits, which made the task a lot easier. They drove straight to the casualty entrance of St. Martin's Hospital, where the man with the broken finger got out.

'I'll stick with him and perhaps you'd go after the other two. You will be careful, though, won't you Claire? Don't leave the car and whatever you do, don't let them see you; I'd much rather you lost them straight away than that.'

'Don't worry, I won't do anything

stupid. Good luck. See you back at the flat.'

Claire did not in fact have very much further to drive; the two remaining men went straight to Waterloo Station, left the Ford in a parking place in the service road and made off in the direction of the underground. She sat for a moment in the car, thinking that she really ought to go back to the hospital to help Mike, but she needed to do some hard thinking before seeing him again and decided to go to the flat. Once there, she ate her share of the picnic lunch and tried to forget all about it by doing some washing and ironing, but it didn't work; however hard she tried to tell herself that it was unnatural, the fact remained that she had never in her life felt so aroused. It wasn't only what had happened by the lake that afternoon, it was the culmination of all the events of the preceding few days.

It was only now that she fully appreciated what had been wrong with her relationship with her husband Bob. She had been pathetically ignorant and inexperienced when she had married him and by the time she had done some reading and talked to a few friends, the pattern of their marriage had become established and it was too late to do anything about it. Looking back on it now, though, she realised that there never would have been a chance of changing him and that they had been fundamentally and completely unsuited in that way. He had always treated her like a piece of Dresden china and his idea of something really daring was to leave the light on. Surely Mike Craven wasn't in the same mould, or worse, not interested either in her or women as a whole. It had been bad enough having to sleep in the same flat as a man whom she found so attractive with only a thin wall separating them, but having to strip naked in front of him and those thugs and remembering what they had threatened to do to her, excited her almost beyond endurance, even though she had been terrified and revolted at the time.

And then there was the mystery surrounding Mike. He was obviously a professional driver and had had an operation on his head, and although a phone call to her brother, who was an avid follower of motor sport, would almost certainly have cleared it all up, she felt it only fair to leave it to him to tell her in his own good time. Having been married to a surgeon, she had inevitably picked up quite a bit of knowledge of medicine, particularly in the accident field and knew the dangers he had run when he had rescued her on those two occasions. She admired his courage enormously, but why hadn't he made any physical approach to her? He had had enough opportunity in all conscience; could it be that he didn't find her attractive? There was one other possible explanation, but she didn't think it was the correct one. Although she was abysmally ignorant of that particular subject, she didn't think he was a homosexual; there was no trace of effeminacy in him and although she realised that that didn't rule it out, his whole attitude towards her had been quite different from that of the only man like that whom she knew well.

Claire paced around the flat in her agitation and even a cool bath — that standby of overheated adolescents, or so she had been led to believe — made things no easier. While she waited for him to return, she went over the scene she had planned hundreds of times in her imagination and when she heard the key in the lock, she got up to meet him, her mouth dry with nervous anticipation.

4

The two hours after the man with the broken finger disappeared into the casualty department of St. Martin's Hospital tested Craven's patience to the full. He sat on the low wall bordering the churchyard on the opposite side of the road facing the main entrance and tried to ignore the hunger pangs which were a constant threat to his resolution to stay put.

Craven could only assume that they had had to give the man an anaesthetic to set his finger, because it was nearly four o'clock before he reappeared and there were a number of occasions when he thought that he must have left by another exit and he nearly made the decision to abandon his vigil. Eventually, though, the man did come out of the main casualty entrance, looking pale and shaky and after blinking for a moment or two in the bright sunshine, hailed a taxi. Luckily for

Craven, there was a whole line of them, no doubt waiting for the end of visiting time, and he got into the next one, getting a good deal of childish amusement out of being able to utter, for the first time in his life, that immortal phrase 'follow that cab'.

The man must have had enough for that day, and be feeling pretty woozy into the bargain, Craven thought, because he made no attempt to cover his tracks. The taxi drove directly to Battersea and he went straight into one of the flats that had obviously only just been completed. They were arranged in two storeys and occupied the whole length of the street, access to the individual front doors of the upper layer being by way of a balcony, and Craven had no difficulty in pinpointing the one in question accurately, even though he could not actually see the number, his job being made easier by the fact that the man had to come down again to pay the driver.

All the way back to Claire's flat, Mike Craven was worrying about her. Now that he had identified the place where the man, who was obviously the leader, lived, he wished he had told her not to bother about the other two; if they had caught her following them, he knew that he would never forgive himself.

The taxi driver's ill concealed expression of irritation at being asked to find change for a £10 note was rapidly replaced by one of total astonishment when Craven airily waved his hand in a dismissive gesture and went up the steps of the block of flats without looking back — he'd not often had the opportunity of being extravagant with someone else's money and it gave him very considerable pleasure.

When Claire met him at the door, relief at the fact that she was safe gave way to puzzled awareness of the difference in her; she was tense in a way that seemed quite foreign to her and normally such a good listener, she obviously hardly took in a word of what he was saying when he told her what had happened after he had left her.

'How did you get on?' he asked when he had finished.

'How do you think?'

There was a faint flush on her cheeks and her tone of voice was so unlike that to which he had become accustomed that for one awful moment he had the suspicion that she had been drinking.

'What's that supposed to mean?'

'After what I went through by that lake, you leave me all by myself for hours demonstrating what a clever he-man you are and then you have the nerve to ask me how I got on. Anyway, it was a stupid idea of yours to get me to go after them; you should have known that I would lose them. I took all that risk for nothing.'

Craven very nearly apologised, but felt the anger welling up inside him at the unfairness of her remark. Why should he apologise? He had saved her twice from being beaten up or worse and this was the only way she could thank him. He very nearly told her there and then just what he thought of her, but made one last effort to control himself.

'I'm tired and I'm hungry,' he said, his voice shaking with suppressed rage, 'let's discuss it later.' He got to his feet and started towards the door.

'Where do you think you're going?'

'To have some of that picnic.'

'You'll be lucky.'

Craven stared at her, but she met his gaze without looking away, a mocking smile on her face.

'I ate it all and if you think I'm going to get you anything else, you've got another think coming. This isn't a hotel, you know.'

Craven ground his teeth together. 'I'll find something in the larder.'

'And whose flat do you think this is?'

'Claire!'

She put her tongue out at him and this gesture, small though it was, infuriated him even more. He was tired, he was hot and sweaty, he was famished and earlier that afternoon, he had been scared half out of his wits; he felt his heart beginning to pound and took several steps towards her, his nails digging into the palms of his hands.

'I don't pretend to know what's got into you, Claire, but you're asking to have your backside tanned.'

She let out a snort of derision. 'I'm shaking with fear — in the first place you wouldn't dare and in the second, I don't suppose you'd know how.'

Craven fought to keep control over his temper, but the contemptuous expression on her face was the last straw; he gripped her hard by the shoulders and started to shake her violently. Instead of trying to struggle free, she pressed her mouth hard against his and then his control snapped completely as he felt the sudden sharp pain as she bit into his lip. He pushed her roughly down on to the rug in front of the fireplace and threw himself on top of her, tearing wildly at her clothes.

★　★　★

A long time later, as they lay side by side, Craven stroked her gently on the cheek with his forefinger and Claire opened one eye and smiled at him sleepily.

'I don't know why I ever said that I couldn't imagine you getting distraught.'

'Yes,' she replied dreamily, 'I did get rather carried away.' She ran one finger over a large bruise on her thigh. 'You didn't have to be quite so rough, you great bear.'

'But I thought that was the whole idea.' Claire blushed scarlet and he laughed, determined to keep it light. 'Don't worry, I didn't realise it at the time — I'm not that good an actor — but you were quite right.'

'What do you mean?'

'If you hadn't provoked me into losing my temper, the ice would never have begun to melt, let alone be broken.'

'You must think I'm mad or something.'

'Why should I?'

Claire shook her head. 'It just never occurred to me that you might understand.' She leaned across and kissed him. 'I tell you what, I'll make a pact with you; I'll try to explain my side of it to you, if you tell me who you are and why you've been trying to help me.'

'Fair enough, I ought to have done so long ago.'

Craven held absolutely nothing back and Claire listened in silence until he had finished.

'Of course I ought to have explained about Penny before, but at first it didn't seem appropriate and then I suppose I was too selfish to do so; I liked being with you and the fact that I was doing something useful for a change was a wonderful boost to my morale. That night when you were attacked was the first time I had done anything really positive since the accident, but you can have no idea how close I was to running away and leaving you. No doubt you recall how like a jelly I was afterwards.

'I was also terribly mixed up over my physical feelings towards you, which must sound pretty ridiculous coming from someone of my age. On the one hand, I wanted you desperately, but on the other, I couldn't get my guilt feelings about Penny out of my mind. Finally, and to make matters much worse, I had no confidence in my ability to make it if I did try; not only was I afraid that you would turn me down flat — I had the feeling that you wouldn't want to with someone as old as me, not to mention the dirty great hole in my head — but I also thought that that side of my life was over for good — Penny and I did try a couple of times after the accident, but on each occasion it was a hopeless failure. In fact, I'm pretty certain it wouldn't have worked just now if you hadn't pulled that trick on me; as it was, I didn't have time to think or have doubts, emotion just took over. Believe me, I realise that I haven't played fair with you; I should have told you all this when we first met and if you want me to leave, I will.'

'Mike, you can be awfully pompous at times; don't be such an ass, of course I understand that you still have a responsibility towards Penny. You don't seem to realise either just how much you have helped me too and I don't mean only for having saved me from those men this afternoon and the other day.' She paused for a long time. 'I don't know how I'm going to tell you this, it sounds so atavistic.' She took a deep breath. 'My husband Bob was one of those people who are just too gentle and reasonable. He never used to lose his temper, was always on an even keel, saw the best side of everyone and quite frankly, it got a bit too much of a good thing at times, particularly in bed. You may have difficulty in believing it, but we were both virgins when we got married and although this may work out perfectly well for lots of people, it didn't for me. I found the whole thing about as exciting as a constant diet of vanilla blancmange. It was invariably the same routine, which for me got drearier as time went by; it was bed, lights out, all over in a minute or two and then into a dreamless sleep — at least for him. I wasn't a complete ignoramus — I had read a bit and talked to a girl friend about it — and I did try to take the initiative once, but Bob was genuinely shocked and I was made to feel like Messalina.

'This afternoon by the lake I was absolutely terrified while it was all happening, but I have to admit that while I was waiting for you to come back, I couldn't get the thought of what that man said they were going to do to me out of my mind and . . . I . . . I even wanted you to hurt me.' She looked utterly crestfallen. 'I feel so ashamed.'

'Ashamed! Now it's you who's being stupid; lots of women have rape fantasies.'

'But that's a lot to do with what's worrying me, it wasn't just fantasy — I enjoyed every moment of what you did to me just now; in fact, I've never begun to have an experience like it before.'

'That's because it wasn't the real thing; it was all a bit of play acting, all the better for being pretty realistic, but play acting none the less. I wasn't really going to hurt you properly, or rape you, and I'm willing to bet that you knew it just as well as I did. I must admit that I did genuinely lose my temper for a moment, but I'd never have gone on with it unless you had reacted in the way you did. I'll let you into a secret, too; I've been secretly longing to play the caveman for at least thirty years.'

There was nothing crestfallen about Claire's expression as she got up, just a wicked smile on her face.

'Perhaps a bath and then that picnic,

which incidentally I didn't finish, would be in order and then I have a shrewd suspicion that I have a voyage of discovery ahead of me.'

Craven hadn't led a particularly sheltered life and no one could have said that he was inexperienced, but he'd never met anyone remotely like Claire before; for her, the whole thing was obviously like discovering a new toy. As for himself, it was like shedding half a life-time; he showed her that it all depended on one's mood, that there was a time to be rough, but also a time to be gentle as well, when it could be funny and when it could be serious and that there were other times when conversation could be just as stimulating as physical activity. And throughout it all, he marvelled that anyone as young and beautiful as Claire could actually find him desirable and there was also the realisation that this was only the beginning.

It was not until later, much later in fact, that they got round to working out their next step. Every time that Claire looked at him, she could feel a fit of the giggles welling up within her and it was not until they were having a drink at the pub around the corner that she was able to trust herself to talk sensibly.

'What exactly had you in mind?' she said.

'Well, that man I followed is the only lead we have and we've got to find out who he is and if possible get on to the people who are paying him.'

'That sounds rather a tall order, I must say.'

'I don't know. He was in such a state that I can't believe he was lying about the way they got paid and if the same method is used again, it might give us a chance.'

'But what about the fact that the man doing the ordering wanted to see the results of the beating up himself this time?'

'I've got an idea about that, too. Listen . . . '

The plan he outlined seemed to Claire to depend on rather a lot of coincidences, but although they continued to discuss it for a further hour, neither of them was able to come up with anything better.

Craven woke early the following morning and couldn't help grinning to himself when, on getting out of bed, he disarranged the sheet and saw the bruises on Claire's body. He failed to resist the temptation to take a closer look and pulled the bedclothes further back, rapidly composing his face when she opened her eyes and looked at him accusingly.

'What's so funny?'

'I was just admiring the rainbow effect and thinking that if we go on like this, those men will be out of a job.'

Claire massaged herself reflectively, then got up and inspected the damage in the full-length mirror.

'There must be an answer to that, but at the moment I can't think of one.'

It was only too obvious what answer his body was providing, but he forced himself to leave her and retired into the bathroom.

★　★　★

Their first stop that morning was Craven's flat. He knew immediately they had entered the front room that it had been a mistake for them to have gone there together; Penny's presence in the shape of the large photograph above the mantelpiece was all too obvious and her eyes seemed to be following him around accusingly wherever he went. Claire sensed his discomfiture at once and picked up the phone without looking in his direction.

'I think I'd better give Georges a ring and see if he can take over for a day or two.'

'Hang on a second, it would be much better if I did it.'

'Why? You hardly know him and won't it sound strange coming from you?'

'It's just that for the time being I think it would be much safer if he doesn't know what we're planning to do; if he was aware of the fact that you hadn't really been beaten up, it would be so easy for him to give the game away. It's not as if I need say very much to him in any case, just that you've had a fall, or something like that.'

Claire was just about to make a joke

about him being jealous of the young Frenchman, when she suddenly realised that that might be a bit too close to the mark for comfort, remembering some of the looks that Mike had given him, and abruptly changed her mind.

'Yes, perhaps you're right.'

Craven got through to Georges without difficulty and it was only when he went into the bedroom to look for the National Health wig that he had been given after the operation, that the sight of Penny's clothes in the wardrobe brought home to him just how much she had meant to him at one time and how little he had thought about her in the preceding few days.

He let out a weary sigh and sat on the edge of the bed, looking at the object in his hand; he had always thought that cheap wigs for men looked pretty ridiculous and this one was no exception. He had in fact never worn it and now, when he glanced at himself in the mirror, about all that could be said for it, he thought, was that it made him look different and it did at least cover up the depression in his skull. Claire's hoot of laughter when she saw him was just what was needed to break the spell of self pity and he was feeling much more cheerful by the time they had got back into the car.

They arrived outside the row of flats in Battersea soon after eight a.m. and only had to wait for about forty-five minutes before the man came out of the front door and on to the balcony. Just before he closed it, looking through his binoculars, Craven caught a glimpse of a young woman wearing jeans and wine-coloured jumper and abruptly decided on a change of plan.

As the man walked past them on the other side of the street, Craven noted with deep satisfaction that in addition to the splint on his finger, he was holding his neck stiffly and at an unnatural angle and when he came to cross the road, he had to turn his whole body to right and left when he looked to see if there was any traffic coming.

'It looks as if my guess was right and that he is going to the hospital again, but the chances are that he gave a false name there and rather than follow him, I think I might learn more by talking to that woman in there. Keep your eyes peeled and if he appears again, give a couple of blasts on the horn, O.K.?'

With almost anyone else he could think of, he would have had to go off into a long explanation, but Claire merely nodded and looked up at the row of flats.

'How are you proposing to tackle her?'

'Pretend to be a market researcher.'

'Don't be too long, will you? If he comes back by taxi, I won't be able to give you much warning and it won't be easy for you to get away without being seen — you'll hardly be able to leave by the back door and I wouldn't even be certain that there is one.'

'Righto. You don't happen to have a notebook or any paper in the car, do you?'

' 'Fraid not.'

Craven found what he was looking for at a stationer's at the end of the road and after receiving the thumbs up sign from Claire as he walked back past the car, he climbed the steps on to the balcony and rang the bell of number twenty-three.

5

Lynn Barrett knew that there was something wrong as soon as she saw the expression on her husband's face, even before she took in the fact that he was wearing a surgical collar around his neck and that his finger was in a splint.

'Have you hurt your finger then, Ray?' she said stupidly, knowing even before she had finished speaking that she would have been much wiser to have kept her mouth shut.

'What do you think, you silly bitch? That I'm wearing this for fun? Well, what are you staring at?'

'Your neck. Did you . . . '

The punch took her full in the mouth and she ran sobbing into the bathroom and locked herself in. She knew from bitter experience that it would be no good coming out for at least a couple of hours and she sat on the lavatory seat, nursing her bruised lip and thinking that if she played her cards correctly she wouldn't have to put up with it much longer, but at the same time knowing that if Ray discovered what she was doing behind his back, he would kill her. In the event, she had only been sitting there for about ten minutes when he began to pound on the door.

'Stop snivelling and get me tea. Come on, open up.'

Lynn hesitated, but only for a moment, then shot back the bolt and sidled past him into the kitchen. When she approached the living room fifteen minutes later with the plate of sausages, fried potatoes and beans, Ray was on the telephone and his tone of voice was so different from his usual self-confident, blustering way of speaking, that she stopped to listen.

' . . . but we couldn't help it . . . '

He was almost whining and when she glanced through the crack in the door, she saw him standing there, the telephone several inches from his ear, looking like a frightened rabbit.

' . . . but, Boss . . . '

Even though she was a good ten feet from the instrument, Lynn could hear the angry voice coming from the other end of the line and smiled to herself.

' . . . but I have to be at the hospital at nine . . . very well, boss, I'll meet you here at eleven.'

She waited for a minute or two after he had rung off, then pushed open the door with her foot and put the plate on the table. Normally a voracious eater, Ray only picked at the food and finally pushed the dish away, swallowed a couple of pain killing tablets and went off to the bedroom.

Lynn managed to get through that night and breakfast the following morning without any further trouble by the simple expedient of saying absolutely nothing and doing precisely what Ray demanded quickly and without complaint. When he got up it was obvious that he could hardly move his neck at all and a sleepless night had clearly done nothing to improve his temper. As he went out, he paused at the door and with considerable difficulty and obvious pain turned to face her.

'Get this place cleaned up — it's like a pig-sty. The boss is coming here at eleven and it'd better be all right by then. And put a dress on before I get back.'

The man with the dark hair, who had been standing in the kitchen listening to the conversation, waited until he heard Barrett slam the front door, then crept up on the young woman, who was leaning out of the window watching her husband walk up the street. When she felt the hand on the waist-band of her jeans, she jerked her head round and opened her mouth to scream, but then she saw who it was and let out her breath slowly.

'Mind my lip,' she whispered as he covered her mouth with his.

The man drew back and touched it gently with his forefinger. 'We can't waste a convenient visit to the hospital, now can we?'

'But supposing he comes back? He might have forgotten his appointment card or something.'

'You have a point there. You'll just have to go on watching out for him then, won't you?'

The thought that her head and shoulders could be seen from the street added enormously to Lynn's excitement and she gripped the window sill tightly to stop herself from crying out as the man slipped her tight jeans down over her hips. She ground her teeth together and closed her eyes, her breath coming gradually quicker and quicker, then snapped them open again as the sensation, which was so exquisite that it crossed the dividing line between pleasure and pain, shot through her. For a moment she didn't take in the significance of what she could see, then it became obvious that the man on the balcony was coming to her flat; seconds later the front door bell rang.

'Ignore it,' the man whispered fiercely in her ear.

'I can't; he's seen me and he'll be round at the window in a minute.'

'Get rid of him then and for God's sake make it quick.'

Lynn pulled up her jeans and slipped the chain in position before opening the front door a crack.

'Good morning, madam. I'm doing some market research on washing powders and . . . '

She tried to slam the door, but the man already had his foot in position and he gave her a sight of the ten-pound note in his hand.

'There is, of course, a fee, madam.'

Lynn was just about to tell him to go away, when the man tip-toed up behind her.

'Take the note, I want to look at it,' he whispered in her ear.

'There's more where that came from; all you have to do is answer a few simple questions.'

Lynn took the note and handed it to the man, who after examining it carefully for a moment or two, put his mouth right up against her ear.

'Give me a couple of minutes, then let him in and take him into the sitting room — I want to give him the once over.'

She nodded, looking over her shoulder to make sure that he was out of sight and then slowly drew the chain across.

'You won't be too long, will you? My husband . . . '

It was perfectly obvious to Craven that the young woman was scared stiff; there was a hectic flush on her cheeks and he noticed her bruised and swollen lip at once. She was a great deal more attractive than he had thought when watching through the binoculars and also much younger — he didn't think she could have been a day over twenty-five.

'Not to worry, Mrs . . . ?'

Craven raised his eyebrows and at first thought that she wasn't going to answer, but eventually she did, her reply being almost inaudible.

'Barrett.'

'It'll all be over in a jiffy, Mrs. Barrett and then you'll be this much richer.' He gave a conspiratorial wink and raised another of the banknotes. 'Keeps you a bit short, does he then? You'd be surprised how many of them do — one gets to know in my job. Still, what the eye doesn't see . . . If I were you I wouldn't tell him about it and then you'll have a bit more to spend on yourself for a change.

Now, let's see . . . ' He made a great show of flicking through the sheaf of papers on the clip-board and raised his biro. 'Come on, love, cheer up, I won't eat you. What's your first name? Mine's Bill.'

'Lynn.' Again it was no more than a whisper.

'That's a pretty name. Lynn Barrett — I like that. Pretty name to go with a pretty face.'

'You won't write my name down there, will you? Ray'd kill me if he found out.'

'Confidentiality is our watchword.' He raised his biro in the air. 'Now, what make of washing powder do you use, Lynn?'

'Wouldn't you like to come into the sitting room for a moment? It's more comfortable in there.'

Craven looked up sharply, wondering for a moment if she was one of those frustrated housewives he was always reading about in the tabloids, but one look at her face reassured him — she still looked frightened half out of her wits. A visit to the living room was exactly what he did want and he followed her in, trying to think up some reasonable questions.

He kept them as short as he could and hoped that his lack of knowledge wasn't as glaringly obvious as it felt like to him.

It was only too clear that with every passing minute fear was winning the battle with her desire for the money and he wasn't happy himself to stay there a minute longer than necessary now that he had got the information he wanted. As soon as he decently could, Craven got to his feet and held out the second ten-pound note, adding a third on sudden impulse.

'Thanks for your help; I didn't mean to scare you and I hope that this will be some compensation. Don't move — I can find my own way out.'

The man in the kitchen pushed the serving hatch open a few more inches.

'Has he gone?'

Lynn nodded and went across to the open window, leaning out as she had done before.

'He's on the pavement now.'

'Good. Keep an eye on him, but don't make it too obvious and give me a running commentary on what he's getting up to — there is a little unfinished business I have to attend to.'

If it had been exciting for her before, it was ten times more so now.

'He's getting into a Mini parked up the road — there's a woman in the driving seat . . . Oh!'

'What's up? Has he ripped his trousers or something?' Lynn gave a giggle and the man gripped her even more tightly. 'Keep still, for God's sake. What are they doing now?'

'Just chatting, that's all. Why did you want me to get him inside the flat?'

'I thought I recognised his voice when he was at the door and I wanted to make sure. For your information, those tenners belong to Ray.'

'What?'

'They were part of his last pay packet. It may also interest you to know that that bloke wrote down your phone number and nicked one of Ray's pipes.'

'Why should he want to do that?'

'After his fingerprints, I expect.'

'Who is he?'

'You've no need to worry your pretty

head about that. Are you still watching that car?'

Lynn let out a choking gasp. 'I'm trying to.'

* ★ *

Ray Barrett felt a complete idiot with the more elaborate collar they had fitted him with at the hospital, but he had to admit that he was much more comfortable with it on and at least his finger was much less painful. To add to his anxieties about what the boss was going to say, he was late and the man was an absolute stickler for punctuality. To his relief, though, he seemed to be in the best of tempers; he was standing staring out of the window and whistling to himself quietly.

'How's the neck then, Ray?' he said without looking round. 'You can thank your wife for the fact that I forgive your lateness — she's been very hospitable, very hospitable indeed. Oh, by the way, the geezer who bust your finger is in that car down there. Careless of you to let him follow you home, wasn't it, and just as

111

well that I decided to come in by the back way? You're losing your grip, Ray, and I don't employ people who are slipping. Half a minute, though, our friend is getting into that phone box down there; you don't suppose that you're going to be the lucky one, do you?'

Barrett just stood there; the boss always had had a peculiar sense of humour and for the life of him he couldn't understand what the man was talking about. At the sound of the phone bell, though, his jaw literally fell open.

'Well, aren't you going to answer it?'

'What shall I say?'

'Find out what he wants, you stupid git, and let me listen in. Lynn, fetch me a piece of paper and a pencil and put a jerk into it.'

Barrett waited until the man was ready and then lifted up the receiver. 'Hello.'

'How's the finger?'

Barrett's reply was unprintable and the man by his side nodded his approval.

'Cut that out and listen. Have you contacted the man who gave you the orders yet?'

Barrett glanced at his companion, who shook his head.

'No.'

'Good. Look, I know your name, where you live and I've also got your fingerprints from that shotgun, which is a good enough beginning. Now listen; when you get the instructions about how you are to receive your payment, you will ring this number and tell me about it. I'll leave it to you to imagine what'll happen if you don't. Is that clear?'

'But I told you, the bloke said he wouldn't pay at all unless he saw the results himself.'

'You won't need to worry about that — I'll be responsible for seeing to that side of things.'

Barrett looking questioningly over his shoulder, but before there was time for any response, there was a click and then he heard the dialling tone.

'And what was all that about?'

'You know I told you that he had my neck trapped in the car window?' The other man nodded. 'Well, he wanted to know who had given me the instructions and on the spur of the moment I said that I had never met him, that the orders were given by phone and the money left in a briefcase in a hotel room.'

'Where on earth did you get that crazy idea from?'

'I saw something like it in a film once.'

'You're not quite such a fool as I took you for. Now, be quiet for a minute — this situation has definite possibilities.' He paced round the room while Barrett looked at him bemusedly, and then finally came to a halt in front of him and poked him in the chest with his forefinger. 'Look here, Barrett, I'll give you one more chance to deal with this bloke and that woman, but if you mess it up again . . . Now, this is what I want you to do.'

* * *

'How did it go?'

Craven told Claire about the phone conversation. 'So it's just a question of trusting to luck and hoping that I've scared him sufficiently to ensure his co-operation and then seeing what sort of miracle Cynthia Taylor can work on you.'

'Why so glum then? We've made some progress at last and I think you did a terrific job with that woman.'

'She's the one I was thinking about; she's only a kid really and scared stiff of that bully of a husband of hers, who obviously hits her about. I had to make things worse by overplaying the part of the lecherous door-to-door salesman and then finished up by giving her far too much money because I felt sorry for her.'

'How much did you let her have, then?'

'Thirty quid.' Claire let out a low whistle. 'Don't worry, it wasn't mine — poetic justice, really, it was just part of the wad I took off Barrett by the lake.'

'I shouldn't worry too much, if I were you; things aren't always what they appear on the surface. Some people actually enjoy being hit about occasionally, you know.'

'So I've noticed.'

Claire put her tongue out at him and the spell was broken, but even so, he had to turn away so that she didn't notice the tears which were starting to his eyes.

Right from the start, he had tried as hard as he knew how not to blame everything that happened to him on the accident, but there could be no doubting that it had made him much more emotional, and he still hadn't got used to the change.

Although he wasn't aware of it, Claire noticed it at once and decided to change the subject. 'What do you suggest we do next?'

'Ring Morruzzi and get him to call another meeting, you present your features, which by then will be suitably battered, and I'll be there to see how they all react.'

'I still find it difficult to believe that that girl Cynthia is going to be able to make me up well enough to deceive anyone looking at me really closely.'

'Don't you believe it; she's an artist at it and no one will be expecting it to be a fake.'

'But what exactly are you trying to achieve by it? Apart from anything else, you seem to be assuming that one of the members of the association is behind it all.'

'Not only do I think that that is in fact the only reasonable explanation for what has happened, but it will be an admirable way of testing out the theory. In any case, even if I'm wrong, it should persuade Morruzzi that the time has come to tell the police.'

Claire didn't see it in the same light at all and the potential complications seemed endless, but Mike was obviously in a highly emotional mood and it clearly wasn't the best moment to start an argument with him.

'Perhaps you're right,' she said. 'By the way, when is Cynthia coming?'

'Tomorrow morning — as near as possible to the time of the meeting.'

'What about the rest of today?'

'Well, you'll obviously have to lie low at the flat and I think I ought to go along to the Nursing Home — there are one or two details I have to get sorted out with Dr. McAlister.'

Craven had no intention of going to see McAlister, but he did need some time on his own to mull over the problem once more and went back to his own flat. It smelt musty, so he threw open the windows and lay back on the sofa, staring at the ceiling.

The more he thought about it, the more convinced did he become that the threats to the others were just a cover-up; after all, nothing had happened to any of them and it seemed very strange to him that Claire should have been the one to be singled out on the two occasions. She seemed so certain that there was no one who bore her a grudge and yet, if that was true, why had Barrett said that the man giving the orders had wanted to see the results of the beating-up himself. If Barrett had been telling the truth — and Craven was certain that he had — it suggested that the man behind it was a sadistic psychopath and if that was true there might well be no rational reason behind his desire to hurt and humiliate her. Although Claire obviously did not agree with him, Craven felt more than ever certain that the person responsible was someone close to her — no other possibility made sense.

Could one of them be trying to run her

out of business? But who would be interested in a tiny concern like hers — it was such an individual place with a very limited clientele and surely no threat to any of the others. Claire and Georges were . . . Craven sat up suddenly and was so disturbed by his sudden thought that he even failed to notice that it was the first time since the accident that he had been able to get up quickly without being overcome by vertigo. Georges, yes Georges; was it really such an absurd idea? Claire had said that the Frenchman wanted to set up a restaurant of his own in London and he had thought right from the outset that there was something odd about the way Georges behaved towards her, even though he hadn't been able to put his finger on precisely what. Craven glanced at his watch; if he took it slowly, he would be able to arrive at the restaurant while they were clearing up after lunch.

Tessa, one of the young waitresses he had got to know quite well, let him in.

'We were all so sorry to hear that Mrs. Markham was ill,' she said, giving him a welcoming smile. 'Is she getting on all right?'

'Yes, thank goodness. She should be back in a day or two. Everything O.K. here? Not run off your feet, I hope.'

'We would have been if there had been anyone but Georges in the kitchen — he's been super.'

I bet he has, Craven thought. No doubt the man had been having a field day with two attractive girls at his beck and call.

'Here,' he said, 'let me give you a hand.'

'Thanks.'

Georges was scouring a pan when he took the heavily laden tray through into the kitchen.

'Oh hello, Mr. Craven. I wasn't expecting to see you. How's Mrs. Markham getting on?'

'Not too well, I'm afraid.'

'Oh dear. What's wrong with her? Nothing too serious, I hope.'

Craven looked at the man for a moment without speaking, trying to make up his mind what to say.

'She had rather a nasty fall and hurt her face.'

Georges drew in his breath sharply. 'Poor woman — I'll call in to see her tomorrow.'

'I don't think she's ready for visitors yet.'

'Surely Mrs. Markham herself is the best judge of that. You seem to be forgetting that she and I have been working together for a considerable time now. How long is it that you have known her yourself?'

Craven stared at the slight, dark Frenchman for a moment or two without saying a word and then walked out of the kitchen with the empty tray, realising only too clearly that he had made a complete hash of his talk with the young man. He hadn't intended to get involved in a slanging match and it didn't help him at all to realise that he had come out of it worst, nor that precisely the same thing had happened with Carlo.

He helped the two girls to finish clearing and relaying the tables and when the dish washers had been loaded, he paused at the kitchen door.

'Do you think you'll be able to manage

on your own for the rest of the week, Georges?'

The chef turned away from the stove, nodded briefly and then went on with what he had been doing. Craven decided not to make things any worse than they were already and went back into the dining room where Tessa was just putting on her coat.

'Going to catch your bus?'

'Yes, that's right.'

'I'll walk down with you, if I may. It's on my way.'

'O.K.'

'You know about the threats Mrs. Markham has had, don't you?' he said as they waited by the stop in Shaftesbury Avenue.

'Yes, she told us all about it right at the beginning and said she'd quite understand if any of us wanted to leave, but of course none of us was prepared to let her down.'

'Hasn't it worried you all a lot?'

'Not really. Anyhow, it's no good giving into that sort of thing, is it?'

'No, I think you're quite right, but it

must be a bit scary nevertheless. Anyway, you've got Georges to look after you.'

The girl suddenly pressed her lips hard together, made a dive for her handbag and sneezed violently into her handkerchief, holding it to her face for a good two minutes. When eventually she took it away, the tears were streaming down her cheeks.

'So sorry,' she said in a choked voice, 'some saliva went the wrong way. Oh look, there's my bus coming now.'

Craven walked slowly back to the restaurant, trying to drive out the disquieting thoughts that were chasing each other round his head. When he got there, he found the place deserted, with all the lights out and when he tried the door, it was locked. He realised that he could hardly have expected anything different and began to make his way slowly back towards Claire's flat. He very soon changed his mind, knowing that in his present state of mind he might say or do something stupid and so, as he had done so often in the past in times of stress, he took refuge in physical exertion, walking down towards the embankment at a brisk pace.

Once again it worked and by the time he was in sight of the block of flats an hour later, he knew for certain that the only reason he had got so worked up was the simple fact that he was jealous. It didn't make it any better to remember that he had felt exactly the same way about Carlo and he made a firm resolution to snap out of it. Craven was just about to cross the road when he saw the slight, dark figure run down the steps from the entrance and set off down the street. Even though he was at least a hundred yards away, he recognised the man at once — it was Georges.

Craven felt the shock deep in the pit of his stomach; no wonder Tessa had hardly been able to stop laughing out loud at the pathetic figure he must have cut to her — she must have known what was going on all along. What he had been half suspecting for some time must be true and to think that Claire had taken him in hook, line and sinker with all that stuff about him being the only man in her life since her husband!

Without any clear plan in mind, he went after the young Frenchman even though his legs were aching and his feet were sore. At first, Craven thought that the man was going to go back to the restaurant, but a few hundred yards short of it, he turned down a narrow passage-way and disappeared through an entrance.

When he walked past a few moments later, Craven saw that there was a short flight of steps leading down to a pair of green doors and although the light was dim, he could just make out the plastic plate with the faded legend 'The Paradise Club' and underneath 'Members Only.' He hesitated at the top and was still standing there indecisively when a very large man, wearing a leather apron and carrying a crate full of empty beer bottles, pushed his way through the door. When he saw Craven, he put it down and looked up enquiringly.

'Can I help you?'

'I was looking for a gambling club called 'The Ace of Hearts'; someone told me it was somewhere along here.'

The man scratched his head. 'Never heard of it. Why not ask at the Casino? It's that way, just round the corner; you can't miss it, it's got a neon light above the door.'

Craven thanked him and just as he turned to go, caught sight of the name on the side of the crate: 'MAIER'S BIER-KELLER.' He found the main entrance in the road parallel to the passage and all at once realised that Georges' presence at Claire's flat might have an entirely different and altogether more sinister significance. At that time of the after-noon, there was no hope of finding a taxi and he hurried back to the flat as fast as his rapidly stiffening legs would take him, ran up the stairs and let himself in with his key.

As soon as he was inside, Claire put her head around the kitchen door.

'Oh hello, Mike, how did you get on? You're just in time for a cup of tea. Hang on a second and I'll bring it through into the sitting room.' She suddenly noticed how short of breath he was. 'Mike, whatever's the matter?'

'Claire, it's Georges.'

She listened in silence while he told her about his visit to the restaurant, how odd he thought the Frenchman's behaviour had been and how he had found him coming out of the block of flats, after which he had followed him to the club at the back of Maier's bierkeller.

'And so, you see, they must be in it together — there's no other possible explanation. They're obviously both out to put you out of business.'

Claire looked at him for a long time before replying. 'Oh dear,' she said eventually, 'you'd better go through into the sitting room.'

What on earth's that supposed to mean, Craven said to himself. He didn't need to be reminded that Claire was a cool customer, but even so, her muted, even casual, reaction to his news was a shattering anticlimax and while he waited for her to bring the tray in, his feelings of resentment towards her began to simmer again.

Claire said nothing until she had poured out the tea and handed him his cup. 'But

Mike, I thought you knew about Georges.'

'Knew what?'

'I'm not quite sure how to put this, but shall I just say that although Georges is a brilliant chef, he is rather an emotional person and masculinity isn't exactly his strong suit.'

'But I saw him pawing you in the restaurant the other day — I wasn't imagining that.'

'Mike, you can be awfully dense at times — anyone would think that you'd led a sheltered life. Georges wasn't 'pawing' me, as you put it, he just likes to touch people; it's one of the ways by which he communicates and there are lots of other men like him, who are not afraid to display their emotions in that particular fashion, unlike some I could mention. Poor Georges was born the wrong sex. He wouldn't hurt a fly for one thing and I'm extremely fond of him for another, so you have no cause either for suspecting him of having designs on my business, or for being jealous of him.'

'But what was he doing here and at Maier's place?'

Claire let out a long suffering sigh. 'I haven't convinced you, have I? After you'd told him I'd been hurt — which, incidentally, was an extremely stupid thing to have done without letting me know first — he rang up to find out how I was. Luckily I had the presence of mind to put him off coming to see me as I knew that it might spoil tomorrow's plan, so he just left these lovely flowers with the porter downstairs. Now you tell me how many men, unless they had an ulterior motive, would have been thoughtful enough to do something like that.' She got up and rearranged the red roses in the cut glass vase and then came over to him and gave him a kiss on the forehead. 'So you see, there's no need to worry your head about Georges, or Werner Maier for that matter — he's been very kind to Georges and runs a 'gay' club behind his bierkeller.'

'Why didn't you tell me all this before?'

'I thought it might shock you and on top of that, what Georges decides to get up to in his spare time is entirely his own affair.'

Craven smiled ruefully. 'I can see it all

now and all I can do is apologise humbly and say that I'm both relieved and also thoroughly ashamed of myself. I hardly have the courage to admit it to you, but I've spent half this afternoon thinking that you were having an affaire with Georges and the other that he and Maier were plotting to put you out of business. You know, Claire, I badly need someone like you to kick me up the backside from time to time when I behave like this. No wonder young Tessa practically ruptured herself trying not to laugh when I was waiting with her at the bus stop.'

'Why was that?'

While Craven was telling her, she began to get a fit of the giggles and he went across to where she was sitting and took her in his arms.

'You know what happens to girls who make fun of their elders and betters, don't you?' he said as she gradually managed to get control of herself.

Claire gave him the look that he had grown to recognise. 'No, show me.'

6

The following morning, the nearer the time came for Cynthia Taylor to arrive, the more ridiculous did the whole idea seem to Claire, but after the previous evening, she knew only too well that Mike's emotions were not fully under control and she decided to go through with it. Her first impressions of the young woman who eventually appeared, staggering slightly under the weight of a large black case, weren't exactly favourable either; she was half an hour late, her hair was in urgent need of a wash and she kept giving Mike Craven fawning looks, like a dog which was expecting a kick in the ribs, but had been given a pat on the back instead. Claire turned after she had been introduced and went into the bedroom, grimacing ruefully at herself in the mirror, realising that Mike hadn't got a monopoly in the jealousy stakes.

Craven watched the two women disappear through the door, remembering how he had met the small, untidy girl, who had such an uncanny ability to alter people's appearance. About a year before his accident, Craven had been one of the technical advisers on the motoring sequences to a film company on location in North Africa and he'd even had a small part in the production himself, which had involved being made up with horrific facial burns. He had marvelled at her skill — the results had been a little too close to home for his peace of mind when he had seen some of the rushes — and afterwards, as she seemed lonely, had made a point of chatting to her whenever he happened to run across her.

He couldn't remember now what they had talked about, but he had got to know her well enough to realise near the end of their stay that she was terrified about something. Craven knew about fear; it had been his constant companion on the race track and over many years he had observed its effect both on himself and others. Cynthia was afraid, he had no doubt at all about that; all the signs were there, the ceaseless flickering of a muscle under her right eye, the pallor, the tremor of her hands and voice and the unnaturally fast pulsing of the artery in her neck. There was also a desperation about her on that final day's shooting and when it was over he followed her as she left the set.

He stopped her a few yards from the water's edge when it became obvious that she was going to walk straight into the sea. For a moment, when he put his hand on her shoulder, she looked at him as if he was a complete stranger, then quite suddenly she broke down and he lowered her to the sand, holding her in his arms and letting her cry.

It was the sort of tale that Craven had read about often enough before in the more lurid of the Sunday papers, but that didn't make it any easier to listen to. A boyfriend in London had asked her to collect some samples of Turkish delight, a consignment of which he was thinking of importing, from a confectioner in the town. The two boxes did indeed contain

Turkish delight, but also a large quantity of heroin, or so she was told by the plain clothes men who arrested her. The choice was simple; did she want to spend the next twenty years in gaol, or would she prefer to work for six months in a club owned by a friend of theirs?

The men removed her passport, took her fingerprints and gave her twenty-four hours to think about it. They hadn't even bothered to soften the details of what she would be expected to do at the club; certainly, they appreciated that a girl like her might find it disagreeable, extremely unpleasant even, but what was that compared with having to spend the whole of her youth in prison? Cynthia hadn't needed to think about it for long; both alternatives were intolerable and there was only one way out.

Craven had found Cynthia's gratitude embarrassing — it wasn't as if he had even had to do anything very much. The producer of the film, who was also his motor racing sponsor, had contacts in the highest places and as he explained later, the honour of the country was at stake and the traditional Arab reputation for hospitality had been sullied, not to mention an important arms' contract, which had been put in jeopardy. Not, of course, that anything so indelicately direct had ever been mentioned; a good many cups of strong, sweet coffee were drunk and after much convoluted discussion, Cynthia's passport was returned and Craven, when given the option, decided that he would rather not hear what had happened to the policemen and the club owner. The girl had said at the time that if she ever needed his help in any way, she would drop anything she was doing and come at once. She had kept in touch with him, she had visited him when he was incarcerated in hospital and now she had been as good as her word.

Craven had already seen Cynthia's work at close quarters and knew that she was an artist, but, although he was expecting something good, when Claire reappeared at the living room door an hour later, he sprang to his feet and stared at her open-mouthed.

'Good God!'

He went right up to her and inspected her carefully; the effect was just as good close to as it had been from a distance and there could be no doubt about it, Claire looked the most terrible mess. Her nose was thickened and turning blue; her left nostril looked as if it had been slit through and as if the two stitches, surrounded by dried blood, were holding it together; both eyes were blackened and there was another long bruise along the angle of her jaw, which also looked swollen and lopsided; a jagged cut, also with stitches, went from the corner of her mouth towards her cheek and there were a number of splits in her lips. Finally, to complete the horror, three angry-looking burns, which looked as if they had been inflicted with a cigarette end, were visible at the neckline of her dress.

'How do I look?'

Claire's voice had an odd muffled quality to it and it was obvious that she was having difficulty in moving her jaw properly.

'Absolutely frightful!' He backed away

136

and looked at her again. 'Cynthia, you're a genius. How long will it last?'

The young woman gave the nervous laugh that he remembered so well. 'It should be quite secure for the rest of today, but if you want to keep it going for longer than that, I'll have to come round and touch it up for you.'

Craven carried Cynhia's suitcase down to her car and tried to pay her out of the remainder of Barrett's money, but she wouldn't hear of it. She gave him a quick kiss on the cheek when he opened the car door for her.

'Give me a ring if you want me to call in tomorrow morning; I'm working on a series of commercials at the moment and it wouldn't be any trouble.'

'Thanks a million.'

'I hope it does the trick.' She gave him a wistful smile. 'You're beginning to look much more like your old self, Mike — even better in some ways, I'd say.' She looked up over her shoulder towards the flat. 'She's nice.'

Craven watched the car out of sight and then slowly climbed back up the stairs. When he got back to the flat, he had an even more careful look at Claire's face and even then it looked sickenly convincing.

'Isn't it desperately uncomfortable?'

'Not too bad. There's quite a lot of padding outside my teeth on this side — I gather it's the same stuff that dentists use for making impressions — and also up my nose; that's why my speech sounds so funny.'

'What about eating?'

'Cynthia said it would be all right provided I avoid anything too hot.'

Claire got up and went across to the mirror, turning this way and that and smiling to herself.

'What on earth's the matter with your leg?'

'She gave me a small pebble to put in my shoe and a rather fine bruise just below my knee to go with it.'

To his utter shame, Craven began to feel his eyes starting to moisten and, of course, Claire noticed it at once.

'What's wrong, Mike?'

'It's just that it looks so horribly real

and I suddenly thought how close it came to being true.'

'You're an old softy.'

She went to take him in her arms, but they both remembered her face almost at the same moment and he had to take humiliating refuge in the bathroom until he had regained control over himself.

★ ★ ★

The closer the time drew near for them to go to the meeting at Morruzzi's restaurant, the more convinced did Claire become that play acting would only lead to further and unnecessary trouble. If the police were called in, how could they possibly explain their reasons for the elaborate charade? She also shuddered to think what the other members of the association would say and do if they found out. There were many occasions when she was within an ace of voicing her doubts, but Mike had seemed so pleased with his idea and he had already done so much to help her, that she didn't have the heart to do so.

They deliberately left their entrance into Morruzzi's small dining room until everyone else was seated and when eventually they did go in, the hum of conversation was instantly stilled. Claire limped in on Craven's arm, looking like the woman on one of those very old 'Keep Death Off The Road' posters. She had found a black hat with a veil, which she had bought for her aunt's funeral five years earlier, and also had on a black coat and skirt to go with it. She sat down with exaggerated care and when she had done so, Morruzzi cleared his throat and slowly got to his feet.

'Mrs. Markham telephoned me yesterday with some disturbing news and I felt it right to call another meeting.'

Perhaps not surprisingly, Craven thought, he didn't say that he had violently opposed the idea when they had put it to him and that their threat of going to the police independently had been the one thing that had made him change his mind. The last thing that Craven wanted was for the man to get too firmly into his stride, as once that happened there would be no stopping him and half the dramatic impact of Clare's appearance would be lost.

'I think Mrs. Markham should be allowed to speak herself.'

Before Morruzzi could get another word out, Craven helped Claire to her feet and was standing right beside her when she reached up first to lift up the veil and then to remove her hat. She stood there for a moment quite motionless apart from little twitching movements around her mouth.

'I . . . I . . . '

It was a marvellous performance; she half choked on the words, let out one cry of anguish and then her body was racked by great choking sobs. Craven led her out of the room and after giving her a reassuring wink, went back into the dining room.

'And now will you go to the police?'

On this occasion, after he had given them a lurid description of what might so well have happened in reality, there was a little more support for his suggestion, but one of the Cypriots began to trot out the same reasons for not doing so and after letting the argument continue for a few minutes, old Morruzzi held out his hand and gradually silence descended on the room.

Craven had to admire the force and magnetism of the man's personality; he looked round at everyone in turn, fixing his unblinking eyes on each individual until either they looked away or began to fidget with embarrassment, and then began to speak slowly and clearly.

'No one is more sorry than I am that such a terrible thing should have happened to Mrs. Markham and I propose that we organise a collection to compensate her — I personally will make a substantial contribution.' There was a muted chorus of agreement. 'Appalled though I am by it, there is one bright side to it; if this gentleman will give Carlo here a full description of the men involved, I have no doubt at all that we will find them on this occasion. I will not tolerate violence in this area.'

He went on in the same vein for a good five minutes, which gave Craven the opportunity to look round the table again. He didn't learn much; Meswani seemed even more terrified than he had before, if that were possible, Maier from the bierkeller sat there as stolidly as he had done throughout the proceedings and the group of Cypriots and Maltese were shifting about uneasily on their seats, casting furtive glances at one another and occasionally whispering excitedly.

Craven was anxious to avoid anyone either getting too close to Claire or starting to question her and insisted that he was present when Carlo met them after the meeting had broken up. His second impression of the young man was just as unfavourable as his first; he still had an almost irresistible desire to boot him up the back-side, but managed to control himself sufficiently to give a detailed description of Claire's attackers.

'Do you know any of them?'

'Not from what you've told me so far,' the young Italian replied, examining his immaculately manicured nails with great care, 'but we'll work on it.'

'How long is all this going to take?'

Carlo raised his shoulders slightly. 'Who knows?'

The man's supercilious manner was altogether too much for Craven. 'I'll give you exactly three days to do something positive about this and if at the end of that time nothing has happened, we'll go to the police and no doubt they'll want to know why your uncle and the others haven't reported the threats that were made to them.'

Carlo wasn't in the least put out. 'I don't think somehow that that would get you very far.' He smiled. 'What threats had you in mind?'

'You know very well.'

'My dear Mr. Craven, none of the members of our association, with the exception of Mrs. Markham, of course, have received any threats.'

'You may think that you've got all of them under your thumb, but when it comes to it you'll see how wrong you are.'

'If you're thinking of Meswani, you can think again — he'll do precisely what he's told. Now, relax, my friend and leave it to me — I know exactly what I'm doing.'

Craven was beginning to get really annoyed and before he said or did anything foolish, he took Claire by the arm and they left with what dignity they could muster.

'Did you learn anything useful?' she asked when they were out of sight of the restaurant.

'Not much, I must confess, apart from confirming my intense dislike of young Carlo — after he'd got over the initial shock of your appearance, I had the strong impression that he was laughing at us.'

'You mustn't take him too seriously — he's just enjoying being the centre of attention. Normally, I don't think he's got enough to do; his uncle indulges him hopelessly and gives him far too much money. He's never had to take any responsibility and as a result, he's never grown up. Did you get any reaction when I did my unveiling act? I thought it would be safer not to look around too much.'

'It was pretty disappointing, I'm afraid. Morruzzi looked genuinely shocked, I thought that Meswani was going to faint,

Maier's expression didn't change one iota and the Greek and Cypriot contingents just started to jabber at one another.'

'What about Carlo?'

'If it wasn't ridiculous, I'd have said that he found it amusing; it was almost as if he knew that you were made up.'

It was only too obvious to Claire that Mike was quite incapable of thinking straight where Carlo was concerned and she decided to change the conversation.

'What's next?'

'We'll just have to hope that our friend Barrett contacts us and if he doesn't, it'll be a straight choice between seeing what Carlo and Morruzzi turn up and having another go at the police.'

'How good do you think the chances are of him ringing?'

'Not bad, provided he has something to ring about. If he does, one thing will be certain and that is that someone present at that meeting today is responsible for the whole thing.'

Craven wished he was half as confident as he had tried to appear. He hadn't forgotten what a fool he had made of himself over Georges and it didn't make it any easier to know that Claire's heart wasn't in the exercise anyhow. He had virtually given up hope of anything coming of what now looked like a pointless charade, when the telephone went at just before nine o'clock that evening.

'It worked,' he said, unable to keep the triumph out of his voice when he came back into the sitting room. 'One of those people at the meeting must be behind it — no one else could possibly have seen you. I knew there was something fishy about the people at those gatherings; I wouldn't be surprised if they were all in it together, with the possible exception of Meswani.'

Claire smiled one of her secret smiles, which was more deflating than any words she could have used.

'What did he actually say?'

'Just that the man who had given him the orders seemed well pleased this time and told him to go to a hotel called the Beauséjour in Bayswater tomorrow morning at eight to pick up the money.'

'How is it going to be transferred?'

'Same way as last time; it'll be left in a room booked in the name of Russell.'

'Mike, I take it all back — you're a marvel. I'll get on to that police inspector right away.'

'You mustn't do that.'

'Why ever not?'

'Because in the first place I can't see them believing our story and all this hard work will have been wasted, and in the second, even if they did, they'd be bound to muck the whole thing up.'

'I don't see why they should.'

'Experienced crooks can smell the law a mile off — that's how they stay in business.' Craven got to his feet and paced around the room, feeling the adrenalin beginning to charge him up — he hadn't felt so alive since his accident. 'No, I'm going straight round to that hotel now and stay there until the said Russell shows up and then I'll follow him. I know those places; money talks and I've still got about eighty quid of the money I took off Barrett.'

Claire didn't share his enthusiasm.

'Mike, I don't like it one little bit. Suppose it's a trap.'

'How could it be?'

'Very easily. Barrett could have been having you on all the time; I never did think that his story made sense — surely no one would agree to do a job and then be paid like that.'

'It's probably the regular method used by the criminal fraternity, I read somewhere that the men really responsible always like to keep in the shadows as much as possible. Anyway, I'm absolutely certain that Barrett was telling the truth down by that lake; not only was he scared silly, but he was more dead than alive and I just don't believe that he would have had either the time or the presence of mind to make up a complicated story like that. Apart from all that, what possible interest could they have in setting up a trap for me — it's you they're after.'

Claire still didn't like it, but she could see that Mike had the bit between his teeth and that there was going to be no stopping him.

'All right, but you won't do anything

stupid, will you?'

'Course not. I'll be back in time for a late breakfast tomorrow morning at the very latest; you stay put here and please don't answer the bell to anyone — I'll let myself in with the spare key.'

'What about my face?'

'Can you bear to leave it as it is until tomorrow morning?'

'Just about.'

'That's the spirit.'

Claire was standing by the window with the light out and saw the slight figure pause by the street lamp, giving a wave with his hand before striding briskly down the road. She remained there for a long time after he had disappeared around the corner, the tears coursing down her cheeks.

★ ★ ★

Craven only had to wait outside the Beauséjour Hotel for a matter of fifteen minutes or so to discover what the set-up was. There might have been a few bona fide guests, but the majority were there for just one purpose and that wasn't just to enjoy their beauty sleep. The place must have been making a fortune, he thought; during the time he was watching, six couples arrived and half as many departed and none of them were encumbered by luggage.

Craven didn't think that even his worst enemy would have called him mean, but he had always been careful with his money, even in his affluent days, and it gave him a distinct kick to be able to flash Barrett's money about, even though, at the rate he was spending it, it clearly wouldn't last very much longer. He didn't waste time with preliminaries and took a ten pound note out of his pocket as he went up to the reception desk. The man with the slicked down black hair didn't look up straight away, but his attention was attracted all right when Craven began to rustle the bank note.

'I'm an enquiry agent working on a divorce case,' he said, distinctly feeling the part in his crumpled suit and dreadful wig. 'I have reason to believe that someone by the name of Russell will be booking in some time this evening . . . '

'If you mean what I think you mean, the answer is no.'

'My client is prepared to be generous.'

He had to go up to thirty pounds in the end and finally even had to start to walk away before the man was prepared to cooperate at all, but after that he could hardly have complained about the man's willingness to help. Not only did he look through the bookings and confirm that there was one in the name of Russell, which had not yet been taken up, but let him have a room for the normal charge on the same floor with the promise that he would ring through on the internal telephone when the people in question arrived. In many ways, Craven would have preferred to stay in the entrance hall, but the man wouldn't have it at any price, saying that it would put off their other clients. It was obvious that he had a point; the foyer was so small that he would have been far too conspicuous.

The bedroom was as anonymous as all those in second rate hotels always are and

Craven reckoned that he could justly claim to be an expert in the matter. With Claire's warning in mind, he gave the place a thorough search, but there were no bogey-men hiding in the wardrobe or under the bed and no listening devices that he was able to discover.

He listened to the radio for a time and made an attempt at reading the Gideon bible, but found it impossible to concentrate and soon after midnight, he took off his shoes, lay down on the bed and drifted off into an uneasy sleep. In his racing days, Craven had always slept soundly and had been difficult to rouse and before his accident the very slight noise from the door would never have woken him, but it did now. He came to with a start, being for a moment unable to place what had done it; he glanced at his watch, saw that it was a few minutes past three and then, just as he turned over, he heard the unmistakable sound of the key being turned in the lock.

★ ★ ★

'He's safely in room 127, Ray.'

Barrett nodded his head with satisfaction and looked round at the other four men in the office behind the reception desk.

'Good! Now, Ron, I want you and Les to deal with this bloke Craven and Bert and I will handle the girl. Jim, you stay here and make sure that that pansy manager stays safely put in his flat. All right? Any questions?'

The large man with the cauliflower ears grinned back at him. 'You want me to croak 'im, Ray?'

'That's what the boss said and for God's sake don't muck about this time; do it quickly and quietly and remember what happened the last twice. He may not look much, but that bloke knows what he's up to.'

The ex-boxer snorted derisively. 'Nothing but beginner's luck — 'e'll never know what's 'it 'im this time. What shall I do with 'im afterwards?'

'You can leave that to Jim, here. You shouldn't have any trouble; that particular room can't be locked from the inside and if by any chance he's barricaded the door, all Jim'll need to do is give him a ring and tell him Russell's arrived — that should bring him out all right. Come on then, Bert, we've got a lot to do.'

Ron Draper never had been over-endowed with brains and more than two hundred fights in the ring hadn't improved the situation, but violence, legal or otherwise, had been his stock-in-trade ever since his childhood and he grinned with pleasurable anticipation as he tested the blade of his knife against his thumb.

'Want any help, Ron?'

'Nah. I could take that geezer wiv one arm tied behind me back.'

Les felt like pointing out that he had not exactly made a success of it last time, but decided against it; the boxer's temper was like a powder keg and one gentle blow from him would be enough to put most men in hospital for a week.

Draper had been a heavy-weight and had put on a couple of stone since his fighting days, but he was still light on his feet and made very little sound as he went along the corridor towards room 127. The master key slipped smoothly into the lock and with only the faintest of clicks it turned and he eased the door open. The hinge gave a faint squeak and the man paused, holding his breath, and then inched it forward again. His hearing hadn't been quite what it should have been for some time and certainly Craven's treatment of his ears had done nothing to improve it; as a result, he was not totally reassured until in the dim light from the corridor, he saw the shape under the bedclothes and the thick mop of hair protruding from beneath the sheet.

When the door was fully open, he tested the point of his knife on the back of his hand, took a firm grip on the handle, strode across the room and in one smooth movement brought the knife down, burying it to the hilt in the region of the man's heart. In the same moment that he realised that there was something wrong with the feel of the knife as it had sliced through the bedclothes, he sensed a movement behind him. He started to turn, but then there was an explosion inside his head and he fell in a crumpled heap on the ground.

Les Walker had always been small and weak and very early on at school had discovered that as he was totally incapable of protecting himself, the only logical thing for him to do was to find someone else to do it for him. It had not proved all that difficult to achieve either; he found many ways of making himself useful to others and he hadn't lost the knack over the years. No order, however trivial or demeaning, was ever queried or turned down with the one exception of physical violence, which he left to others better qualified. People had got used to seeing him around, to his constant availability and willingness to act as messenger and general factotum and finally he had become indispensable because of his real talent, which was his ability to melt into any background. In appearance, he was almost totally anonymous, no one seemed to notice him and he had developed an uncanny skill in following people and remaining undetected. As usual, he was sitting quietly in a corner of the room, saying nothing and doing nothing to attract attention, when the receptionist came back into the office.

'What's happened to that bonehead, Ron?' he said, 'he's been gone all of fifteen minutes.'

'He's a bit slow is Ron — he'll be back shortly.'

'I'm prepared to give him another five minutes and then you'll have to go up and see what's happening.'

Les was about to object, but he didn't like the look of the hotel receptionist, who had a reputation for ill temper and in any case, the pattern of obedience was so deeply ingrained in him that he wouldn't have known how to refuse anyway.

As he went up the stairs a few minutes later, he wished he had been able to find an excuse. As Barrett had said, Craven may not have looked very formidable, but Les had seen him sort out both Ron and Ray quickly enough and no else had achieved that while he had been with the gang. The one comfort he had was the gun in his pocket — a secret which he had shared with no one.

The key of room 127 wasn't in the lock, but the door was an inch or two open. Les looked up and down the corridor and listened, his head cocked to one side, but all he could hear was the steady, snoring breathing coming from inside the bedroom.

'Ron,' he whispered hoarsely, terrified of waking the sleeping man up, but urgently needed the reassurance of the boxer's presence, 'Hey, Ron.'

Trembling with fear, he took the pistol out of his pocket, screwed on the silencer and pushed open the door with his foot. He could see the shape clearly under the bedclothes and the ridiculous wig, which had slipped forwards over the man's face and was partly covering it. The others had been discussing it in the office and he was immediately reassured.

Les fingered the gun, thinking that at last he would be able to show them; small and timid he might be, but he would deal with the bloke who had made mince-meat out of the other two. He advanced into the door-way, took careful aim at the centre of the wig and pressed the trigger.

The gun let out a loud 'plop' and the figure on the bed gave one jerk and then lay still. Les stood there for a few seconds, listening carefully, but the breathing had stopped and he switched on the light, closed the door behind him and stood there, gun at the ready, savouring his moment of triumph.

He advanced slowly towards the bed and tipped the wig back with the end of the silencer. Ron Draper's eyes, a neat hole placed almost exactly between them, stared back at him and he staggered back against the wall, sick with fear and horror.

Les Walker had not lived on his wits for the preceding thirty years for nothing. No one knew he had the gun — for that matter, even if they had, they would never have believed that he would have had the courage to use it — and the only logical thing to do now was to blame it on the man with the wig. He only hesitated for a moment and then picked up the phone.

'Reception.'

'Jim, it's me, Les. I found Ron on the bed in here — he's been shot dead.'

There was a long pause from the other

end of the line. 'There'll be bloody hell to pay for this. I can't leave here, I've got clients arriving the whole time, but at least I'll be able to cover the front exit. The only other way out at this time of night is by means of the fire escape staircase outside and that'll have to be your responsibility. He can only have been gone a few minutes and if you check the doors to it on each floor, you should be able to see at a glance whether or not he's got out already — you have to break a glass-fronted panel to get hold of the keys. If we can only manage to keep him inside the hotel, we can mount a proper search in the morning.'

'What about the back stairs?'

'Don't worry about them, I'll see to it. Now, get a move on, will you?'

It took Les only a few minutes to check all the emergency exits and when he had satisfied himself that they were all securely locked, he went out into the area behind the hotel and with quiet contentment settled down to watch at the base of the fire escape. He was not in the least dismayed by the task and was in fact delighted to escape any involvement with the nervy job of checking the inside; the evening was fine, his patience limitless and his gun was firmly in his hand. If he could get the man with the wig, he thought, his whole position in the gang would change and now that he had used it once . . .

7

Mike Craven was standing at the head of the stairs leading to the foyer when he saw the shadow moving against the wall and seconds later heard muffled footsteps on the carpet; he ran quickly up the next flight and waited just out of sight round the angle of the wall. He got down on to the floor and risked having a look to see who it was; he recognised the man at once as the one who had held Claire that very first evening while the ex-boxer was hitting her. He realised immediately that he would have done much better to have run straight out through the front door before any of them knew what had happened to the man with the cauliflower ears, but he had still been suffering from reaction when the opportunity had been there and now it was too late.

He was still standing there indecisively a few minutes later when he heard an excited shout from below and he started up the next flight of stairs in a blind panic. Pausing at the top, he saw the fire escape at the end of the corridor, but rejected it straight away as being too obvious and took the key, which he had removed from room 127, and put it carefully in the lock of the door immediately to his left. He wasn't really expecting it to fit, but when it turned smoothly he realised that it must be the master key. He waited for a second or two, thinking that if all the rooms were occupied in the way he expected, then the couple inside were going to be in for a nasty shock. As it turned out, he didn't get that far; as soon as he had opened the door the merest crack, not only did he see that there was a light on inside, but the chain had also been applied and hastily, but as quietly as he could he shut it again.

His next attempt proved an even more nerve-racking experience. He forced himself to wait with the door open a fraction, listening for any signs of activity from within while at the same time keeping an eye on the corridor. Finally, he could stand the suspense no longer, pushed the door wide open and stepped inside; to his enormous relief, he saw immediately that the room was unoccupied and the bed neatly made up, with its cover still in position.

The room was a duplicate of the one he had previously occupied and it only took him a matter of seconds to confirm what he had expected and that was that there was no way of getting out of the window short of breaking the glass, the frame being made of metal and pivoted in such a way that it would only open a few inches.

Craven sat on the edge of the bed, trying to ignore the feeling of fear deep in the pit of his stomach and making an attempt to take stock of the situation, which he liked less and less the more he thought about it. It seemed most likely that he would at least be safe until the morning — they could hardly search every room in the middle of the night, particularly in an establishment such as it obviously was — but what then? They obviously knew that he was still in the hotel and equally clearly they had been expecting him, which meant that he had been taken in completely by Barrett. He was perfectly well aware that Claire hadn't wanted him to come to the hotel in the first place, but it was a bit late in the day to be thinking about that now.

Craven was still sitting there half an hour later, so preoccupied and cast down that if it hadn't been for the unholy row coming from outside in the corridor, he would undoubtedly have been discovered.

''Keep right on to the end of the road, keep right' ... oops ... gie me a hand, luv.'

They spent such a long time fumbling with the lock that he was able to smooth down the covers on the bed and get into the built in wardrobe with sliding doors before they half fell into the room and through the gap between the doors, he saw a young man with his arm round a girl's shoulders come staggering across the room.

With the Glasgow accent, which you could have cut with a knife, his Tam-O-Shanter and long scarf, it didn't require a genius to tell that he had been trying to drown his sorrow at Scotland's crushing defeat at the hands of England at Wembley Stadium that afternoon. The girl just managed to get him to the bed, where he fell backwards, letting out a series of loud hiccups, while she went across to close the door and then stood looking at him, an expression of cynical amusement on her rather sharp features.

The man tried to sit up, but the effort was too much for him and he collapsed back on the pillows and started to giggle fatuously.

'Come on, then, let's see you. Get 'em off.'

'I won't get anything off until you pay me — I already told you, it'll be twenty quid.'

It was like taking money off a baby. Once she'd relieved him of the notes, she helped him off with his jacket, shoes and trousers 'to make him more comfortable', then disappeared into the bathroom, 'to freshen up'. Five minutes later, when the young woman put her head cautiously around the door, the man was fast asleep and snoring. She had just got her hand inside the hip pocket of the Scotsman's trousers when Craven decided that the time had come for him to put in an appearance. The girl was so engrossed in her task that she didn't hear him until he spoke.

'Having fun?'

Craven thought for a moment that she was going to faint as she whirled round, all the colour draining from her face, but he had to admit that she recovered her self possession astonishingly quickly.

'Who the hell are you?'

'Just someone who wants to get out of this crummy joint in one piece.'

It was obvious that she didn't know what on earth he was talking about and she stared at him with a look of blank amazement on her face. Craven put the Tam-O-Shanter on his head and wound the scarf around his neck.

'I'm going to pretend to be our drunken friend here and you're going to help me get past that bloke in the foyer.'

'And if I don't?'

'I'll wake up 'Sleeping Beauty' here and tell him what you were doing — I don't suppose he'll be all that pleased. If you do help me, you can keep his twenty quid, although, heaven knows, you can hardly claim to have earned it, but if you try any funny business, I'll . . .

He showed her cauliflower ears' knife, but wished she had managed to look a bit more scared. When he had first appeared, she had obviously been momentarily frightened, but now he could have sworn that she was finding the whole thing a huge joke. He could only suppose that, in order to survive, people in her line of business got pretty good at summing up members of the opposite sex and he had little doubt that she had him rumbled.

She looked at him for a long time before replying. 'All right, I'll do it for another tenner.'

'Very well, it's a deal.'

Craven took one of Barrett's last remaining notes out of his pocket and held it out.

'Are you a nut-case or something?' She held up the Scotsman's roll of bank notes, which she had been holding all the time, then threw it on to the bed and shrugged her shoulders expressively. 'Well, it's your money.'

Craven felt the tension inside him relax — he quite literally had no idea what he would have done if the young woman had called his bluff; he was quite certain he couldn't have woken the Scot even if he'd tried — the man hadn't stirred all the time they had been talking and it didn't look as if he was going to for many hours yet. Craven started to take off his jacket and trousers and the girl took a step or two backwards.

'If you think . . . '

'Relax, relax. I don't suppose that bloke on the reception desk is completely blind and I'm just going to do a swop with junior here.'

When he picked up the roll of notes from the bed and tucked it into the top of the man's underpants, the girl could hardly bear to see it happen. Craven transferred his own money and keys into the Scotsman's trews and then slid the knife inside the waistband. They were a pretty tight fit and although he could just do up the button at the top, he had second thoughts after having taken a step or two across the room; if he was going to have to run, the knife would undoubtedly do him a serious mischief and in any case he didn't like the beastly thing and knew perfectly well that he'd never be able to use it whatever the circumstances. He pulled it out again and slung it on to the bed.

The young woman had been watching his antics with an expression of utter amazement on her face. 'Now I know you're a nut-case.' She shook her head in disbelief. 'You can't leave that thing there.'

'Why ever not — I don't like knives.'

'Look, mate, that geezer downstairs knows me — I take this room on a regular basis — and if things don't go right I may need an excuse for having helped you, see? You held a knife on me, so I didn't have much choice. It could be that he'll have a hard enough job believing me anyway, but if you leave that bloody thing on the bed . . . '

To his shame, Craven hadn't thought of that side of things at all and realised that their Scottish friend could hardly have been expected to slink out in the morning without creating some sort of fuss.

'I'm sorry, it was stupid of me; it's very kind of you to be helping me anyway — I can see that I'd better leave everything to you. What do you suggest?'

'I don't know; one minute you're threatening me if I don't help you and the next you're thanking me for something I haven't done yet.' She raised her eyes to the heavens. 'I don't know how you came to be involved with this lot, but I'll tell you this, you won't last long at the rate you're going — the blokes you're up against aren't nice at all and they're pros.'

'Who's the boss of this set-up?'

'Even if I knew, which I don't, I wouldn't tell you; I just use this place because it's convenient. Now, I can't stay chatting all night — are you coming or aren't you?'

'I'm all yours.' Craven picked up the knife and made a fencing pass at her. 'Lay on Macduff.'

The young woman gave him a look of withering contempt. 'Now don't go and get carried away by that haggis eating image of yours and for God's sake keep your mouth shut when you get down there; just leave all the talking to me. We'll go down in the lift and when we get out, lean on my shoulder, keep your head down and . . . '

'Shut up?'

'You seem to have got the message at long last.'

Despite it all, Craven couldn't resist a loud hiccup as they came staggering out of the lift, which earned him a well deserved dig in the ribs.

'That was quick, Linda. Couldn't he make it then?'

'What does it look like? Open the door for me, will you? Unless, of course, you'd like to get rid of this gonk for me.'

'You know I'd do most things for you, Linda luv, but there are some limits.'

Craven waited until they were well away from the hotel and then unwrapped the scarf from round his neck and pulled out the remainder of Barrett's money. There was about forty pounds left and he reckoned she'd earned it.

'I wish it could have been more — if it hadn't been for you I'd have been in dead trouble in there.'

'Don't spoil it — I don't often have the opportunity to do someone a good turn.'

Craven could have kicked himself. He had always been ready to admit that he didn't understand women and if he'd needed a reminder, this was it.

'I'm sorry, it's just that I took the money off one of the heavy mob in there a day or two ago and I didn't see why you shouldn't have some of it.'

Her expression softened a little. 'In that case . . . '

He handed the notes across. 'Do you mind if I ask you something?'

She let out a deep sigh. ' 'What's a nice girl doing in a job like yours?' ' she said in a 'stage' voice. 'Well, in the first place I'm not a nice girl, in the second I like doing it and lastly, if I hear that question just once more, I'll scream.'

'No, it's not that, it's just that I didn't realise it when I asked you, but you're running a big risk in helping me and I was just interested to know why you did it.'

'You don't have to worry about me — I can look after myself.'

'But what'll happen when they find that Scotsman in the morning? That bloke in the foyer will never believe that you were forced into doing it — you were far too natural about it — and believe me, there's going to be an unholy row when they find out that I've escaped.'

'You didn't think I was going to leave our Scottish friend in the lurch, did you? And him with all that lovely money in his pants.' She opened her handbag and held up a key. 'There's more than one way in and out of that hotel, you know, and Jim goes off duty at eight.'

'Why in that case, didn't you let me out with your key and then slip back in — then no one would have been any the wiser.'

'Because the way happens to be through the manager's flat. He never minds me using it, but somehow I thought he'd draw the line at you as well. I provide some rather special services for him from time to time and even if I do wake him up on my way back, which I

175

have no intention of doing, the poor fool will actually be grateful.'

'But how will you get that drunken Jock out?'

'The lift stops in the manager's flat and when he goes on duty in the morning, I'll make use of that convenient fact.'

'But suppose the tartan wonder creates a fuss?'

'He won't — I'll give him a good time just before we leave and believe me, that'll take his mind off anything else.' She laughed when she saw his expression. 'I told you I wasn't a nice girl.'

'You still haven't answered my first question.'

'You mean the reason why I helped you.' Craven nodded and she looked him up and down for a few moments before replying. 'Just let's say that I like the look of your ugly mug, shall we?'

'Whatever the reason, I'm very grateful.'

Craven gave her a hug and planted a kiss on her cheek and from her reaction believed that just for once he had actually done the right thing.

'Don't be soft,' she said and he could

have sworn that there was a catch in her voice.

* * *

Meswani had not been able to get the mental picture of Claire Markham's face out of his mind ever since the meeting at Morruzzi's restaurant. He had always been a timid man with an absolute abhorrence of violence in any shape or form and he had been close to being physically sick when he had seen what had been done to her. Even before that, the threat to his beloved Kiren and the two boys had almost made him decide to sell up and move away and now, he no longer had any doubt that this was what he was going to have to do. If he had had any relatives in England, he would have sent his family away long ago, but they were all in India and it would take time to organise.

Ever since he had received that first terrifying phone call, he had put bars inside the ground floor windows and bolts on the front and back doors and

177

that night, he took particular care to ensure that everything was secure and only then did he go up to bed. In anticipation of yet another restless night, he had taken a couple of sedative tablets an hour earlier and almost at once fell into an uneasy sleep.

Meswani's terror was compounded by his state of confusion as rough hands ripped back the bedclothes, a brilliant light was shone straight into his eyes and while he was still struggling to shake off the effects of the drug he was bundled down the stairs and into the back room. The man with the metal splint on his little finger hit him brutally across the face with his good hand and then pushed him back into the easy chair.

'Wakey, wakey,' he said loudly and then raised his hand once more.

The Indian flinched and licked his dry lips. 'What do you want?'

'Just a little cooperation. You are going to ring your friend Mrs. Markham and get her to come round here.'

'But why?'

'That needn't concern you, little man.'

'But she's been hurt badly and I couldn't possibly . . . she won't be well enough to come.'

'She'll come all right if you say the correct things and you'd better make a good job of it, my friend, or else . . . Bert, go and fetch the girl.'

'No! Please, no!'

'Shut up.'

Meswani sat shivering in the chair while the other man was out of the room and then let out a cry of anguish when he brought the slight, strikingly beautiful Indian girl into the room, holding both her arms behind her. Her long, glistening black hair cascaded over her shoulders and she blinked uncertainly in the bright light as Barrett got up and stopped in front of her. He licked his lips, whistled appreciatively and then hooked his fingers into the neck of her long white nightdress, pulling down sharply; the thin material ripped throughout its whole length and the girl began to whimper in distress, turning her head away in fear and shame as the man looked her up and down.

'It's a pity that they always seem to go off so badly when they get older,' he said reflectively, 'but at this age . . . ' He turned towards Meswani, who looked as if he was about to collapse completely at any moment. 'You will telephone Mrs. Markham and tell her that your daughter has been raped; she has not been badly hurt and there is no need for her to go to hospital, but she is in a great state of distress and you are too scared to go to the police and in any case you don't think that would be in the girl's best interests — you know what would happen; there would be medical examinations, lengthy questioning — it would all be too much for her. You have no female relatives or friends and she is the only person you can turn to. Get the idea?'

Meswani failed to reply, sitting in his chair, rocking back and forth and moaning softly to himself. Barrett took a couple of steps towards him and lifted him up by the coat of his pyjamas.

'We haven't got all night and you'd better make it sound convincing — if you don't, we could always make your task easier. Hey, Bert, perhaps that's not such a bad idea; I'm sure his nibs doesn't like to tell lies and perhaps if we were to do it here in front of him, he'd make a better job of it.'

He ran his thumb nail down the length of the front of the girl's body and laughed coarsely when she recoiled and started to cry. Meswani made one pathetic attempt to go to her rescue, but Barrett pushed him back contemptuously with one hand and then, taking a firm grip on the man's ear, led him into the hall and lifted up the telephone for him.

'Here, allow me. I'll even dial the number for you and you couldn't ask for better service than that, now could you?'

Barrett waited until the sleepy voice answered and then handed the instrument across, gesturing meaningfully towards the back room from whence they could still hear the girl sobbing loudly.

★ ★ ★

Claire Markham had always been a heavy sleeper and it took her a minute or two to

181

understand what Meswani was talking about, but once he had calmed down sufficiently to explain, she did not hesitate.

'Of course I'll come. What's your address?'

It was only when she had finished dressing that she remembered the conversation she had had with Mike Craven earlier in the evening just before he had left for the hotel. It would be a bitter irony if, having warned him about a trap, she were to walk into one herself. All Indian accents sounded the same to her and suppose the call had just been a device for getting her out of the flat?

She found Meswani's number in the book without difficulty and felt more than a little guilty when the man replied immediately, imploring her to hurry. She could hear Kiren crying loudly in the background and having promised that she would start straight way, left a note for Mike Craven and took one last look at herself in the mirror. Whatever Meswani said, she was proposing to go to the police immediately she had seen Kiren and that meant that she was going to have to clear up her face, but that would have to wait; Meswani's daughter was only fifteen and the way she was handled in the next hour or two might make all the difference to whether she became mentally scarred for the rest of her life or not.

The Indian lived in a detached house just beyond Camden Town and Claire was there within fifteen minutes. She ran up the short flight of stone steps, the keys of the Mini in her hand and rang the bell. Meswani opened the door almost before she had taken her finger off the button and she saw the anguished expression on his face.

'Mrs. Markham, don't . . . '

She caught sight of the dark shape behind him, hesitated for a moment, then turned to run. The large man, who had been waiting at the base of the steps behind her, let out a coarse laugh, twisted one of her arms up behind her and clamped a massive hand over her mouth. The moment he took it away again, she opened her mouth to scream, but before she could take a proper breath, an evil-smelling sack was pushed roughly over her head, a length of rope was wound around her waist, pinioning her arms to her side, and although she kicked out with all her strength, her ankles soon suffered the same fate. She was then unceremoniously bundled into the back of a car parked just around the corner and Meswani was left watching from the door, tears streaming down his cheeks.

On several occasions in the preceding few days, Claire had known what it was like to be frightened, but those experiences had been short and sharp and over almost before she had had time to take them in fully. Now, in the dark, with the foul-smelling sack over her head and trussed up in the back of the car, she had an hour and a half in which to think about what was going to happen to her. This time there would be no Mike Craven to rescue her and even though she was sure that he would go straight round to Meswani's house when he found her note, he would still have no means of knowing where she had been taken.

She could only assume that the men

were the same as the ones who had tried to beat her up before, but she had no more than this to go on; she hadn't seen either of them clearly, they hadn't uttered one single word in her presence and nothing happened to interrupt the smooth progression of the car. When eventually she heard the crunch of the tyres on gravel and they came to a standstill, her back was stiff, all the feeling in her feet had long since disappeared as the result of the tightness of her bonds and her face felt sore where the rough sacking had scratched her skin.

The two men carried her out of the car, up some steps and then she was lowered to the floor. In the distance and too far away for her to catch any of the words, she heard a hum of conversation and soon after she was picked up again. This time, they ascended two flights of stairs and moments later, they came to a halt, the cords around her waist and ankles were severed and the sacking was ripped roughly off her head.

Claire blinked in the bright light and could not suppress a shudder of fear when she recognised Barrett with his splinted finger held out in front of him.

'The boss wants to talk to you, but first you will take a bath in there — you have exactly half an hour in which to get ready. By the way, he also said you were to take all that stuff out of your mouth and off your face.'

Barrett put the blade of his knife inside the neck line of her blouse and slit the material all the way down to her skirt, then very slowly and with exaggerated care, cut off the rest of her clothes. When she was quite naked, he stepped back and looked down at her, laughing coarsely as she tried to cover herself up.

'Well, get on with it.'

'I can't walk; my feet have gone to sleep.'

'You'll have to crawl then, won't you? No, not like that, on your hands and knees. My, that's a fine set of bruises — you seem to have carried realism a bit far, I must say. You can wash those off as well.'

Claire began to make her way painfully across the bedroom carpet, having to endure the humiliation of Barrett's mocking laughter and the shame of her degrading posture. When finally she got to the bath, she sat on the lino with her back to it, massaging her feet, and when the circulation began to return, she had to grit her teeth to stop herself from crying out as the intense pins and needles began to spread. When eventually she did manage to climb into the bath, Barrett sat on the bidet nearby, staring at her and picking his teeth with his knife. Claire did her best to ignore him, soaking in the hot water and deliberately avoiding looking in his direction. He didn't speak again until she had finished drying herself and was standing in front of the mirror removing the plastic moulding from inside her mouth.

'I thought I told you to wash that stuff off your legs.' She flinched as he prodded her hard with his forefinger. 'Hey, Bert,' he called out loudly when he had inspected her skin more closely, 'come and see what this fine lady and her fancy bloke have been getting up to — disgusting I call it.'

The two men looked her over as if she had been a prize heifer and she could do nothing to prevent the blush that spread all over her body.

'All right,' Barrett said, when he had tired of the sport, 'your time's up; put this on and come with us.'

Claire wrapped the dressing gown around her and followed the two of them down to the sitting room on the floor below. The young man, who had been sitting in an easy chair and smoking a cigar, got to his feet as she came through the door.

'Carlo!'

He saw surprise in her expression, which rapidly turned to a look of utter contempt; there was certainly no respect in it and not a trace of fear. He drew in his breath so that the tip of his cigar glowed red, thinking that that would come later — there was plenty of time and it would after all have been disappointing if there hadn't been plenty of spirit to be broken.

'Sit down, my dear Claire.' He motioned the two men out of the room and waited until the door had been shut behind them. 'You won't mind if I call you that, will you?'

'If it amuses you, you can call me anything you like, but whatever your game is, you won't get away with it — we're not in Sicily now, you know.'

The young Italian knocked the ash off his cigar with one sharp tap of his forefinger. 'I'd advise you not to try to annoy me; it might even work and that would only serve to make it much worse for you.'

'All right then, what do you want?'

'You, my dear Claire.'

'Grow up, Carlo.'

'You were unwise enough to have said that to me once before,' he said slowly. 'It was about a year ago — remember that time in my uncle's restaurant?'

Claire did. She had been on a visit to see Morruzzi about her wine stocks and Carlo had taken her up to his office in the lift. When he had stopped it between floors, the young man had pushed her roughly against the wall, started to kiss her and put his hand under her skirt. The

Italian boy — even in age, he was hardly more than one — had genuinely expected her to give in not only without any resistance, but even with gratitude that she had been selected for his attentions. She had not even been frightened to start with — she was even amused — but when she had laughed at him and told him not to be stupid, he had produced a knife and she suddenly realised that he wouldn't hesitate to use it. It had not been a very lady-like thing to do, but she had pretended to cooperate, which allowed her to get a very firm grip on a particularly vulnerable part of his anatomy.

Carlo's humiliation had been complete; he had even finished by pleading with her not to tell his uncle. Perhaps, in the long run, it would have been better for him if she had — anything would have been preferable to the way she had treated him.

'Don't be silly, Carlo,' she had said, 'there's no need to bring your uncle into it. Isn't it about time you grew up, though? You're a nice looking boy — why not find a nice girl of your own age?'

She had adjusted her blouse, pressed the button to restart the lift and when it came to rest, calmly turned her back on him and walked out. Insane with rage, he had snatched up the knife, which had dropped to the ground, and took one step forward, but then he saw his uncle waiting for her at the end of the corridor and punched the control panel savagely with his fist, crying with anger and frustration as the doors closed and the lift began to descend.

He met her again a day or two later and although superficially she behaved quite naturally, he could see that beneath the façade, she was laughing at him. More than anything in the world, he wanted to see that cool exterior shattered, but he decided to bide his time, knowing that the wait would increase his pleasurable anticipation. The second time he saw her, he apologised humbly and went out of his way to be agreeable to her; whenever there was a meeting of the association, or she came to see his uncle, he continued to be polite and respectful, but all the time he was planning his revenge.

Carlo looked at her through the smoke of his cigar. 'To begin with, I was merely going to teach you a painful lesson and make it look as if it was all part of a protection racket, but when those fools twice made a mess of it, I had a much better idea. You made an unpleasant remark about Sicily just now. Do you know what happens there sometimes? A rejected suitor will sometimes kidnap the girl, make love to her and after that, marriage becomes accepted. I am not going to force myself on you, but, believe me, before long you are going to beg me to do it to you.'

Claire looked back at him steadily. 'That first time, in the lift, I made the mistake of thinking that you were just a young boy in a foreign country, who had just got a bit carried away. Now I know you for what you are; you're a sadistic psychopath, Carlo, and the only way you'll ever make love to me is if I'm unconscious.'

The young Italian walked across to the fireplace and pressed the bell, then paced up and down until Barrett and the other man came back.

'She's being stubborn. Tie her up against the racks in the cellar; there are some rats down there and we'll see how she feels after twenty-four hours or so in the cold without anything to eat or drink.' The two men pulled her roughly to her feet. 'Before you go. take off her dressing gown and lift her arms in the air. Now, perhaps this will give you something to think about down there.'

Carlo drew in hard on his cigar again and, staring straight into her eyes, pressed the end firmly into her left arm-pit. Claire drew in her breath with a sharp hiss and the muscles of her chest and shoulders contracted violently, but she did not utter another sound even though he kept the cigar there until it went out and it was Carlo who dropped his gaze first.

8

By the time he got back to Claire's flat, Craven was feeling light-headed with a combination of physical fatigue, lack of sleep and reaction to his series of narrow escapes, but all this was forgotten when he found her note. He read it through carefully several times.

'Meswani's daughter has been raped and I have gone round there to see what I can do to help. DON'T WORRY — I rang him back to make sure that it really was him and not a trap. Hope all went well with you. Love, Claire.'

Craven didn't like it at all; surely it was too much of a coincidence for it to have happened just when he was at the hotel. He found Meswani's number in the telephone directory and the Indian answered at the first ring.

'It's Michael Craven here. I was very sorry indeed to hear about the dreadful thing that happened to your daughter; is she all right and is Mrs. Markham there? I'd very much like to speak to her, please.'

'I don't know what you are talking about, sir. My daughter is quite well and I have not seen Mrs. Markham since that meeting — poor lady, she was so badly hurt.'

'But look here, man, I've got a note here from Mrs. Markham saying that she had gone round to your house.'

'I am sorry, sir, truly I am, but Mrs. Markham is not here. Please, sir, it is four o'clock in the morning. Good night.'

It took Craven ten minutes to get a reply from an all-night taxi rank and another twenty to reach Meswani's house in Camden Town. Claire's Mini wasn't in sight and he ran up the flight of stone steps and pressed the bell. When there was no reply, he went down to street level again to look up at the windows and it was then that he caught sight of the piece of metal glinting in the moonlight. He walked across and bent down casually to see what it was and then dropped to his haunches and picked up the bunch of keys. Within a matter of moments he found the Mini parked round the corner and returned to the house. This time he started to flip the covering to the letter box in and out, finally opening it wide and shouting through.

'Come on, Meswani, open up. It's me Craven — I know you're in there and if you don't come by the time I count to ten, I'll wake up the whole neighbourhood. One — two — three — four . . . '

He heard the sound of footsteps and then the door was opened a few inches on its chain.

'Why don't you leave me alone, sir. I've not done anybody any harm.'

'Look, Meswani, I know you're scared, but I also know that Mrs. Markham's been here — I found the keys of her car by your front steps.'

The Indian slowly undid the chain and stood there looking utterly defeated.

★ ★ ★

Lynn Barrett had always been a light sleeper and when the door-bell rang, she was awake instantly. Her first thought was

196

that it must be Ray — even though he had told her that he was going to be away for the night, it would be just like him to come back unexpectedly. He always had been as jealous as hell and he had taken to testing her in all sorts of ways recently.

The door was on its chain and this was no doubt the reason why he had rung, or, she thought, perhaps he had lost his key. She gave up the idea as soon as she came within sight of the door; Ray would long since have been shouting for her through the letter box. She stood there in the hall, her heart thumping wildly, and nearly jumped out of her skin when the bell went again and the flap on the letter box was pushed open. The deep voices from outside carried through quite clearly.

'Anyone in there?'

'I don't know, sarge — I can't hear anything.'

'All right, let's give 'em a couple more minutes and then we'd better have that door down. Has Len had time to get round the back yet?'

'Yes, I waited for him to get there before ringing the first time.'

Lynn had heard enough and opened the door a crack.

'Who is it? What do you want?'

'Police. Drug squad. Open up, please.'

Lynn had heard tales from Ray about the drug squad and knew that not only had they no need to get a warrant, but that they were quite capable of carrying out their threat of smashing the door in.

'Just a minute — I have to put my dressing gown on.'

Lynn ran into the kitchen, snatched up the biscuit tin containing their supply of grass and carried it through to the bathroom where she flushed it down the lavatory. In the quiet of the night, the cistern seemed to make an appalling noise, but it was too late to be worrying about that and she hurriedly went back to the kitchen having washed the tin out and half filled it with raisins from the packet on the shelf.

Her first shock when she undid the chain on the door was to find that there was only one man outside and the second came when he pushed past her, relocked the door and without a word pulled her into the kitchen.

'Sit down, I want to talk to you.'

Without his wig, she hadn't recognised him at first, but when she saw his head and the moment he spoke, she realised who it was and the icy fingers of fear began to play up and down her spine. Keeping one of her arms forced up behind her back, he moved around the room until he found a long length of washing line and then dumped her, none too gently, into one of the chairs. He wound the rope round her chest, pinning her arms to her sides, but leaving her hands free, tied her ankles to the legs of the chair and then sat facing her on the opposite side of the table.

'Your husband has kidnapped my friend, Mrs. Markham and I want to know where he has taken her.'

The young woman licked her lips. 'But Ray never tells me anything — I know nothing about it.'

'I don't believe you. I think you know who I am — you recognised this, didn't you?' He pointed to the depression on his

199

scalp and leaned forward, staring straight into her eyes until she dropped her gaze. 'When I was here the last time, I was wearing a wig and as you've never seen my head before, someone must have told you about it, mustn't they? If Ray never tells you anything, then it must have been someone else. Why were you so scared and yet at the same time excited when I came to see you that morning? I think that there was someone else in the flat. You would never have let on to Ray that there had been a market research man in here alone with you, particularly one who gave you money — he wouldn't have liked that at all and he wasn't in a good mood, was he? He'd hit you in the face the night before, hadn't he?'

'I don't know what you're talking about.'

'I only hope for your sake that you're lying.'

'What do you mean?'

Craven got up and started to look through the drawers and cupboards and after a minute or two, came back with a bottle of methylated spirits and a mincer,

200

which he slowly assembled and screwed to the edge of the table close to where the young woman was sitting.

'I'm not a very nice person,' he said, his low conversational tone making it all the more terrifying, 'and to show you what I mean I'm going to tell you a story. It would be long before your time, but I was with the Palestine Police just after the war. One day, we caught a young girl — she would have been about your age, in fact — and she knew the names of most of the members of one of the terrorist organisations, which was causing us a great deal of trouble. We fed her fingers, one at a time, into a mincer, rather like this one and even then, she didn't tell us. We did many other things to her, too, and finally we poured petrol over her hair and set it alight. She was very brave and she had a cause in which she believed so strongly that she preferred to suffer terribly and finally die rather than betray her comrades.

'I still remember that girl's screams — I always will — and that's why I hope you have something to tell me. I don't think you are anything like so brave as that girl — very few people could possibly be — you most certainly don't have a cause and you owe that bastard Ray nothing. And it's not even as if he need ever know that I've been here. I'm prepared to do every single one of the things that were done to that girl and the only difference will be that I'll have to gag you — I can't afford the luxury of listening to your screams.'

Craven got up, took his handkerchief out of his pocket and when he had moved round the table, gave the handle of the mincer two or three turns.

Lynn Barrett had been listening to the man with mounting horror; if she had been able to reach her ears with her hands, she would have tried to blot out that quiet voice, but it went inexorably on and by the time he had finished, she was sobbing quietly. She didn't doubt for one moment that he would be capable of treating her in the way he had described and she told him everything she knew, while he listened, interrupting only to ask a question from time to time. When finally she had finished, he went out into the hall and she thought he had gone for good, but then he reappeared and she turned her head away and let out an involuntary cry of terror.

'I've fixed the phone in case you're tempted to use it when you manage to free yourself, but don't worry, it'll look like a loose connection in the unlikely eventuality of Ray ever coming back. Now, if you value my advice, you'll clear out and have nothing further to do with any of that mob.'

The young woman didn't seem to be listening and Craven's last sight of her when he left the kitchen for the last time was of her staring into space, a few tears still running down her cheeks.

* * *

Mike Craven had got no pleasure at all out of terrifying the young woman and as soon as he was back in the car, he was already regretting having told her that particular story. He had been nauseated by it himself when he had heard it from

Sven, his co-driver, while they were waiting for the recovery vehicle, having broken their car's suspension during the Acropolis rally one year. The Swede had done many things in his life, but had usually managed to turn up in places around the world where there was violence and excitement; amongst other things he had been in the Palestine Police, a mercenary in the Congo and the professional bodyguard to a number of highly unsavoury characters. Craven had been disgusted by many of his stories, but they had made compulsive listening and he had become morbidly fascinated by them during the many long hours the two of them had spent together.

Once Lynn Barrett had confirmed that Carlo had been the man in her flat that day, Craven had no real doubt about Claire having been taken down to Morruzzi's place in the country. Evidently the old Italian hadn't been there for several years, having left the running of the place to his nephew, and Lynn had been a visitor at the country house on a number of occasions when her husband was out of the way. It was obvious, too, from what she had said, that a good deal more went on down there besides the business of looking after the wine.

Despite all Lynn had told him, Craven still couldn't think what Carlo was up to; according to her, he had pots of money, so what was his aim in involving himself in such a clumsy and inefficient attempt at a protection racket? And why had he been so intent on having Claire beaten up? The thought of what might be happening to her spurred him on and he drove the Mini as fast as he could, which was very fast indeed, burying his anxiety in the skill he knew best.

It was a few minutes after six thirty a.m. when he arrived in the vicinity of the house. Lynn Barrett had hardly been in the best state of mind to give an accurate description of the place, but knowing that it had a long drive leading up to it and large grounds with many trees in them at least meant that the chances were good that his approach would be a relatively simple one.

A milkman starting his round in a

nearby village gave him final directions and he drove slowly past the main entrance. The house was not visible from the road, but he was able to reverse the Mini some distance up a narrow track which wound its way through the wood bordering the grounds. When the going got too rough, Craven abandoned the car and set off on foot, picking his way through the trees and bracken. The wooden fencing enclosing the estate was rotten and had fallen down in many places and he had no difficulty in getting through. Before long, he caught a glimpse of the house and lay down on the ground, surveying it from behind a convenient clump of bushes.

When he was satisfied that there was no sign of life, he went back under the cover of the trees and skirted the side of the house to see if an approach from that side would be any easier — at the front, the drive passed through open lawns and if anyone was watching, they would be bound to see him. A bank of rhododendron bushes at the side of the house ran almost up to the stables, which had been converted into garages, and he was only left with about thirty feet of open ground to cross before he reached them. The doors were open and inside, in addition to a tractor and a motor mower, he found two cars parked there end to end, a FIAT and a blue BMW; the engine of the latter was still warm and after having felt it, he was even more sure that he was on the right track.

Both cars were locked and it was obvious that the quickest way of immobilising them would be to let down the tyres; he had just bent down to loosen the valve of the BMW's near side front tyre with a small pair of pincers that he had found on a shelf, when he heard a sound that brought him back upright with a jerk. The low growl was repeated and the Alsatian laid back its ears and slowly advanced towards him, its legs bent and its body only a few inches off the ground.

Mike Craven had been thinking so much about Sven on the way down, that it was perhaps not so surprising that he should have remembered the Swede's words on the subject of guard dogs.

'They're an absolute cinch,' he had said. 'They're all trained to go for your arm and clothing and once they've done that, it's child's play.'

That was easy enough to say, but quite another matter with a large and vicious dog only twenty feet away and edging closer with every passing second. Keeping his eye firmly on the animal, Craven bent down, making his movements as smooth as possible, and picked up the large piece of sacking which was draped over the motor mower only a couple of feet from him and wound it round his left forearm. As he straightened up, the Alsatian came at him in a rush, burying its teeth in the sacking and its weight caused him to stagger backwards.

If it hadn't been for the car behind him, he would have been knocked flat, but as it was, he was able to steady himself and taking a firm grip on the beast's front paws, he suddenly pulled both its legs sideways until they were parallel with the ground. Craven felt and heard the joints dislocating and with just one strangled yelp, the dog let go of his forearm and when he looked down, he saw that it was dead.

'Not bad, not bad at all — I wouldn't have believed it possible if I hadn't seen it with my own eyes. I don't suppose the boss will be all that pleased, though, he was fond of that animal.'

Craven released the dog, wiped his forehead with the back of his hand and slowly straightened up to face the man who was standing at the door of the garage, a shotgun in his hands.

The man raised the barrel a fraction as Craven took a step towards him. 'It would be a pleasure to let you have it — right in the guts — so no more of your funny stuff.'

Craven was not allowed to get within ten feet of the man and was forced to walk round to the front of the house and then, with his hands clasped behind his neck and the shotgun rammed into his back, through the front door and into the hall. Without taking his eyes off him, the man cradled the gun in his right arm and began to beat the gong on the table with his left hand. Almost at once, a door slammed upstairs and a rough voice shouted down from the landing above.

'Belt up, Bert! What the hell are you playing at?' The man suddenly caught sight of Craven standing in the middle of the hall and began to come down the stairs. 'Ah, Mr. Craven. You're all we needed to make our day complete; the boss told me you would be along this morning and I didn't believe him. He was ever so annoyed when he heard that those fools in the hotel had made a mess of things, but he said you wouldn't be able to keep away from your lady friend and it seems he was right. I must say it is nice to have you two love-birds together; I wouldn't be surprised if it gave the boss some new ideas.'

The man started to back up the stairs, but stopped abruptly when Craven began to speak.

'He's got some ideas about Lynn, too, you know.' Barrett whirled round, all the colour draining from his face. 'I know who your boss is and who do you think told me? I paid your Lynn a visit this morning, you see, and she talked — in fact, I had difficulty in stopping her. I thought I had scared her into silence, but I misjudged her, she must love him more than I thought. She must have rung Carlo up after I left, even though I fixed the phone; how else do you think he knew I was coming? You're a bit slow on the uptake, you know Barrett; Lynn was even having it off with him when you went to the hospital to have your neck fixed that morning. She told me about that, too. He's much better at it than you are — but then, of course, he is a lot younger and he's got a lot more imagination.'

For a moment, Craven thought that he had gone too far as Barrett took several steps towards him, but then the man turned on his heel and ran up the stairs.

* * *

Carlo was just about to press the button on the top of the aerosol tin of shaving cream, when in the mirror he saw Barrett standing at the doorway of the bathroom.

'That bloke Craven's here — Bert's looking after him in the sitting room.'

'Good! That ties up all the ends very nicely indeed.'

'How come you were so certain that he would be coming this morning?'

'It figured.' The young Italian shrugged his shoulders.

'But how did he know where to come?'

'How should I know? We could always ask him — it might provide some light entertainment, particularly if we do it in front of the girl.'

'I already have.'

'Look here, Barrett, what the hell are you playing at? I'm beginning to get just the . . . '

'Lynn told him and that wasn't the only thing she told him either.'

Carlo licked his lips. 'You didn't believe a word that punk said, did you? He's just trying to get us at each other's throats.'

'There's no other way he could have found out and there's another thing; how did Lynn come to know about this place? Tell me that.'

'You must have mentioned it to her at some time.'

'I never told her a single thing about

my job.' The colour began to rise up the back of Barrett's neck. 'Nobody plays about with Lynn and . . . '

He brought the knife up from behind his back and when he took a step forward, Carlo raised the can and pressed the top hard with his fore-finger. A stream of shaving cream took Barrett full in the face and he let out a bellow of agony, lunging forward with the knife and cutting great swathes through the air, but Carlo had already dropped to the ground and was out of the door while Barrett was still trying to clear his streaming eyes.

When eventually he could see clearly again, Carlo was standing in the doorway with a mocking smile on his face. Barrett started to draw back his hand to throw the knife, but he was far too late. The silenced gun in Carlo's hand jerked once and gave an innocuous sounding 'plop' and a black hole appeared in Barrett's forehead. By the time he had hit the ground, a red stain was already beginning to tint the white of the shaving cream.

Carlo went out on to the landing and listened; Bert Francis was a bit thick and had always done what he was told, but he was a particular friend of Barrett and even without that, there were enough complications without him knowing about the corpse in the bathroom. There was no sound coming from below and he crept down the stairs and looked through the crack in the door. Craven was slumped in an armchair, looking totally innocuous and utterly dejected, while Bert was watching him like a hawk, the shotgun at the ready. Carlo tightened the belt on his silk dressing gown and stepped into the room.

'Good morning,' he said, smiling cynically at the cowed figure in the chair. 'Not feeling very talkative at the moment? You will, my dear fellow, you will.'

'What have you done with Mrs. Markham?'

'Patience, patience, give me ten minutes and I will have the greatest pleasure in explaining it all to you. Bert, if he so much as moves a finger, give him a blast in the legs; I've got one or two things to attend to upstairs.'

The young Italian left the room and

Bert Francis sat a little closer to the edge of the upright chair, his finger on the trigger of the shotgun, watching the figure huddled up in the easy chair. The slight man with the large dent in his head didn't look in the least formidable, but he had seen him kill the dog with his own eyes and both Barrett and Carlo seemed to have a healthy respect for him, so he decided not to risk relaxing for a moment.

Bert had been expecting some defiance and at least a show of resistance, but the man just sat there for the next five minutes, hardly moving. Quite suddenly, he gave a little grunt and Francis stiffened, bringing the gun up a fraction more. As if hypnotised, he watched the man's eyes suddenly open wide, then his neck and spine arched backwards and an inhuman cry burst from his lips. He slipped to the floor and his body began to twist and writhe in a series of violent convulsions, until finally he lay inert on the carpet, a trickle of saliva running down his chin and his breath rattling in his throat.

Bert Francis had heard about epilepsy — one of his cousins suffered from it — but he had never seen an attack before and the sight of it filled him with a mixture of horror and fascination. He advanced cautiously, looking down at the prostrate figure. He never even saw the man move, only felt the appalling pain in his groin, and his mouth fell open, he dropped the gun and then doubled up, retching violently. The butt of the shotgun took him on the side of the head and consciousness was mercifully extinguished.

Craven knelt down beside him. The man's pulse was steady and he let out his breath in a sigh of relief; for one terrible moment, he thought that he had killed him. As he began to straighten up, he saw a movement out of the corner of his eye and hurled himself flat; behind him, a china figurine on the occasional table by the side of the fire-place disintegrated and then the door was slammed shut and he heard the key being turned in the lock.

Craven sprang to his feet, levelled the shotgun and fired one barrel; the lock shattered and following a series of violent kicks, the door swung open. He heard Carlo's feet on the gravel outside and just as he got to the front entrance, the sound of the BMW's engine. He didn't stop to think; the young Italian had infuriated him ever since he had first set eyes on him and he had no intention of letting him get away.

Craven was forty-three, he had missed a complete night's sleep and he had taken almost no exercise at all for more than a year and so, even though the Mini was little more than two hundred yards away, by the time he got there, he was feeling nauseated and his heart was hammering away painfully in his chest. Nevertheless, he wasted no time in trying to regain his breath and sent the little car hurtling down the track and on to the road.

If Carlo had had any sense, having had more than a minute's start, he would have been able to lose his pursuer straight away, but the man was scared silly and fear is hardly conducive to the exercise of judgement. A few miles from the house, the road wound up a long hill and no more than eight hundred yards ahead of him, Craven saw the glint of the early morning sun on the blue BMW. As he had hoped and expected, the young Italian was going straight up the main road, back to the place where he would be able to go to ground with his cronies — London, instead of eluding him by using the narrow country lanes.

Even if it had been driven by an expert, Craven would have backed himself to catch the car ahead, particularly on the twisting road, which gave the Mini an advantage, but Carlo wasn't an expert and it was obvious, when he got closer, that the BMW was handling badly. Normally, he knew that that particular model was extremely stable on corners. but through the rear window of the car ahead, he could see how much of a struggle Carlo was having to control it and he suddenly remembered having loosened the valve on the near side front tyre.

Seeing the Mini getting ever larger in the rear-view mirror, Carlo increased his speed and went far over to the right side of the road in order to take the next left hand bend. He saw the milk lorry lumbering towards him only fifty feet away and wrenched the wheel round; the BMW lurched across the road, missing the lorry by inches and as the rear end began to break away, he attempted to correct the skid, but there wasn't enough road and the car mounted the verge and slammed into a tree still travelling at fifty miles per hour.

Craven brought the Mini to a screaming halt and reversed back on to the grass at the side of the road. The BMW had cut a great swathe through the bracken and its bonnet was buried in the trunk of a massive oak tree. If he had been wearing a seat belt, Carlo might well have survived the impact, but as it was, he had been catapulted through the windscreen and hit the tree, lying draped along the bonnet, the top of his skull smashed to pulp. Craven had seen his share of car crashes, but it was all he could do to check that the man really was dead and afterwards, he was forced to sit down on a tree stump and allow the spasms of nausea to pass.

After a few minutes, he got up, wiping the sweat from his forehead and looked up the road. The lorry driver had not stopped and Craven could only assume that on the sharp bend he had not seen the actual crash, or, perhaps more likely, had not wanted anything to do with it. Whatever the reason, it made things easier for him; there was nothing anyone could do for Carlo and having no driving licence, he himself could do without the attentions of the police at that particular moment.

The thought of the police reminded him that Carlo had had a gun and he soon found it on the floor in front of the passenger seat in the BMW. He was just about to pick it up, then changed his mind, when he thought of the possible complications with the police if they did happen to come along and found it on him. He climbed back into the Mini and drove back to the house at a steady pace, pulling up right outside the front door. It looked to him very much as if the birds had flown; the FIAT was no longer in the garage and when he went into the hall with the shotgun at the ready, the only sound was the tick of the grandfather clock.

Craven saw that he had only been out of the house for twenty minutes, but already the cold fingers of fear were playing up and down his spine as he realised that Barrett and the other man would have had ample time to move Claire. When he pushed open the shattered door of the sitting room, the man called Bert was no longer there and he went from room to room, bellowing out Claire's name and getting more and more desperate as he found nothing. The main bedroom was one of the last that he visited and he wrenched open the doors of the wardrobe, recoiling in horror as the dark shape began to fall towards him, hitting the floor with a sickening thud.

Craven turned the body over with his foot, grimacing with distaste as the man's sightless eyes, with the dark hole between them and their garland of shaving cream, stared up at him. He staggered to the basin, willing himself not to start retching and as he felt the cold water on his face, suddenly realised the significance of Barrett's death. Carlo must have killed him and Bert, injured as he was, could never have moved Claire on his own; she must still be somewhere in the building.

It was only when he got back to the hall that he remembered Morruzzi's cellar and that it must be under the house. He cursed himself for a fool and when he found no access from the ground floor, went outside and soon discovered the door, made of solid oak and decorated with iron studs, at the base of a short flight of stone steps at the back of the house. The blast from the remaining barrel of the shotgun had no visible effect and he began to attack it with the hatchet that he found in the garage; it was, though, only really designed for chopping firewood and it took him the best part of an hour to make any impression on the door. Eventually, when his hands were blistered and sore, he felt it give slightly and, redoubling his efforts, he landed a series of frenzied blows on it with the axe. Even then, it required several mighty kicks with the sole of his shoe before it flew open with a tremendous crash.

Craven pressed the switch on the wall just inside and the strip lighting flickered a few times and then came on; he continued down the steps, turned the corner and then stopped dead in his tracks. Claire was tied to one of the racks, her arms and legs spread wide and a strip of sticking plaster across her mouth. He just had time to take in the blackened area in her arm-pit, surrounded by an angry red halo, before he rushed across to her and gently began to peel the plaster from her mouth. He could see the pain in her eyes, but although her voice was hoarse, there was no hint of a catch in it when she answered his question.

Craven was near to tears himself. 'Are you all right? Carlo didn't — I mean he . . . '

'No, that was to come later.'

'What about your arm?'

Claire even managed to raise half a smile. 'I got bitten by a rat.'

9

'It's all right, Mrs. Craven. Try to keep still.'

The voice seemed to be coming from an immense distance and Penny Craven opened her eyes; everything was out of focus and she tried to get her hands to her face to clear her vision, but something was holding her down and her attempt at a scream merely hurt her tongue, which was being forced into the floor of her mouth by the large tube passing down her throat. She thrashed about in terror and then came the sharp sting of the needle in her thigh; she tried to escape the agonising pain as the fluid went in and just had time to recognise the familiar, nauseating smell of the paraldehyde before she felt herself drifting back into unconsciousness.

When eventually she came to again, the tube was out of her mouth, but her throat was dreadfully sore and every swallow was an ordeal. She tried to speak, but all that came out was a harsh croak.

'Try to drink a little of this, Mrs. Craven.'

The nurse lifted up her head and she managed to take a sip of the cool liquid, which even though it hurt did help to ease the foetid taste in her mouth. Gradually, during the course of the day, there were times when she knew where she was and what had happened, but with these lengthening periods of awareness came the horrors on the wall, which brought her out in a cold sweat and rang high pitched cries of terror from her. Even worse, were the voices which whispered insidiously in her ear and forced unwilling replies from her lips.

'Looking like you do, I don't know how you can bear to see yourself in the mirror. What's that? You can't? I don't blame you, not with your stringy hair, scraggy figure and that face! I don't blame you. You are ugly, Penny, when before all this you were beautiful and who do you think was responsible for all your misery? Louder — I can't hear you properly.'

'It was Mike! My husband, Mike!' she shouted at the top of her voice.

'That's better. And what would you like to do to him in return? Pay him back?'

'Yes! Yes!'

'Make him suffer in the same way as you have suffered?'

'Yes!'

'Kill him?'

'Kill . . . kill . . . kill.'

Firm hands pressed her back on the pillows and someone wiped the sweat from her forehead with a flannel, then there was the dull pain of another injection and finally there came merciful relief as it began to take effect.

In the course of the next few days, she made steady progress; the visions and the voices became less intrusive, they were able to take down the intravenous infusion and oral preparations were substituted for the injections. Gradually, as her physical condition began to improve, it started to dawn on her what she had to do, particularly when she realised that McAlister was in the plot too and that this time they were proposing to lock her away. What other possible explanation could there be for the way they were treating her?

'Why don't you let me have my clothes?' she asked him one morning when he came to visit her.

'They're not yet back from the cleaners; they were in rather a mess when you came in, you know.'

'But in that case, why can't my husband bring in some others? Where is he? Why doesn't he come to visit me?'

'Because I told him to stay away for a few days.'

'Why?'

'I thought it would be wiser for him to wait until you were more like your old self again.'

'He's left me — you're just trying to hide the fact from me — he's found another woman.'

'Calm yourself, Mrs. Craven. He's rung up every single day and it was entirely on my advice that he's stayed away.'

'But I want to see him — I've got something very important to tell him.'

'Why not wait for another day or two?'

Penny held back the bitter words that were on the tip of her tongue, knowing instinctively that if she said anything more, her imprisonment would only be made more secure.

'Perhaps you're right,' she said, forcing herself to give him a smile, 'Mike has been through a bad time too. I'll do my best to be patient.'

McAlister was immediately on the alert; she had been so touchy since coming properly to her senses that her sudden reasonable behaviour was too good to be true. Later that day, while the nurse was helping her with her bath even though he couldn't really believe that she had managed to get hold of any alcohol, he personally searched her room from top to bottom. Despite the fact that he found nothing, he still didn't trust her an inch.

Even though he knew perfectly well that Craven couldn't afford it, he arranged for a special nurse to stay in her room the whole time and straight away got on the phone to St. Botolph's Hospital. He felt desperately sorry for the Cravens, but apart from the obvious fact of their financial worries, the Abbey couldn't afford the sort of scandal that a suicide would bring and their security wasn't up to the sort of risk that a patient like her posed. He was still convinced that Craven would be in real danger if he let her go home — many of the things she had said in her delirium made that abundantly evident. His relief when Dobson, the physician in charge of the alcoholic unit at St. Botolph's, agreed to take her in there within the next couple of days was unbounded and he gave strict instructions that she wasn't to be left alone until the transfer had been affected.

Any optimism that Penny had had that they might be going to let her go home was dashed when the constant surveillance continued, even though by this time she was well enough to get up for meals, wash herself and walk about the room on her own. She had been in the Abbey Nursing Home before and even though on those previous occasions she had been in almost as bad a state, she had always been left alone at night, not to mention short periods during the day as well. If either Mike was refusing to come, or, as McAlister said, he was not being allowed to visit her, there was only one thing left for her to do and that was to escape.

Planning a method of getting out of the building occupied all her thoughts and eventually she had an idea, which she thought might just work. With this end in view — and to give her the means to end it all if her plan failed — she began to collect a proportion of the capsules she was given, holding them in her cheek until the nurse's back was turned and then transferring them to the inside of the mattress by way of the small hole she had made with her finger nail. Even though there were times when she was near to screaming point and her body was crying out for the drugs, this was one time when she was not going to give in to temptation and with an immense effort of will, she managed to hold out.

Whenever the opportunity arose, she emptied the contents of one or two of the capsules into the small empty glass pot on the shelf above the basin, which had at one time contained face cream. One evening, she reckoned that she had collected sufficient for her purpose and decided to make her move the following morning. If the usual daily routine was going to be followed, the day nurse would come on duty at eight o'clock, her breakfast would be brought in at about eight-thirty and then, when it had all been cleared away, the two of them would be left undisturbed until McAlister made his rounds at eleven thirty. The psychiatrist was a great man for routine and all the times she could remember never once had he been more than a minute or two early or late and if he kept to his usual time-table she reckoned she should have ample time.

★ ★ ★

'Nurse Rossiter.'

'Yes, sister.'

'I'm putting you in with Mrs. Craven again this morning. She is being taken to St. Botolph's Hospital this afternoon, but we haven't told her anything about it yet as Dr. McAlister doesn't want her upset in advance. You know her as well as anybody and as there's bound to be the most terrible row when they come for her, your help will be invaluable. I only hope we don't have to hold her down and put her out. I hate that sort of thing and the fact that we haven't been able to contact her husband doesn't make it any easier — he hasn't answered the phone for the last few days.'

Margaret Rossiter didn't blame him. She had already done one spell of duty in Penny Craven's room and had found the experience unnerving; the woman had spent most of the time staring at her, hardly saying a word and when she did speak, it was mainly to produce vitriolic outbursts directed at her wretched husband.

The night nurse was waiting with her cape already on when she went into the room and Mrs. Craven was standing at the basin.

'She's all yours and I must say you're welcome to her,' the girl said in a low voice as she passed her on the way out.

'What are you two muttering about? If

you have anything to say, why not say it out loud. You might have the decency not to whisper.'

Margaret Rossiter had to admit that the woman undoubtedly had a point and as there seemed to be no point in aggravating the situation, she decided to take the blame.

'I'm sorry, Mrs. Craven, there's no need to get upset; I was just asking nurse if you had had a restful night.'

'Don't you think it would have been more courteous to have addressed your remarks to me?'

'I can only apologise again; I didn't mean to be rude. What would you like for breakfast?'

'A boiled egg, toast and a mug of strong Bovril. Dr. McAlister is keen for me to have as much in the way of natural B vitamins as possible,' she added pointedly, seeing the nurse's expression of surprise, 'or perhaps you're the one who gives the orders around here.'

Margaret Rossiter picked up the receiver of the internal telephone, gripping the instrument tightly in a vain attempt to keep some sort of control over her rapidly increasing temper and gave the instructions to the kitchen.

'When am I going to be allowed to dress properly? It's so humiliating having to walk around wearing nothing but this ridiculous night-shirt and dressing gown.' The nurse didn't reply and Penny Craven turned on her angrily. 'And you might have the decency not to stare at me when I'm about to start washing — am I not to be allowed the least bit of privacy?'

Margaret Rossiter flushed in annoyance and embarrassment, turning away and looking out of the window until the woman had finished and got back into bed. Soon after, the maid came in with the tray and she sat down, watching while the patient spent the next few minutes obsessionally removing the shell from the top of the boiled egg.

'Nurse!'

'Yes, Mrs. Craven.'

'Where's the marmalade I asked for?'

'You didn't order any, Mrs. Craven. In any case, wouldn't the sweetness be rather unpleasant with the Bovril?'

The woman put her egg spoon down heavily on the plate. 'Are you accusing me of lying?'

Margaret Rossiter muttered a curse under her breath and got out of the easy chair, sighing audibly and thanking her lucky stars that at least she wouldn't have to put up with it much longer. The woman frankly gave her the creeps with her lop-sided face, blood-shot eyes and sharp tongue and she couldn't help thinking that the sooner she was shipped off to a proper mental hospital, the better it would be for everyone.

'If you're going to be like that about it, you needn't bother.'

The nurse glanced round, rapidly losing the battle to control her temper, and watched as the woman in the bed stirred the meat extract and took a cautious sip. Straight away, she put it down again carefully on the tray and stared at the nurse until she looked away in embarrassment.

'You've put poison in my drink. Who gave you the orders? My husband, or was it McAlister?'

'Don't be so silly, Mrs. Craven — no one is trying to poison you.'

'I can taste something in it and I know that all of you have been trying to get rid of me.'

She sat there slowly stirring the Bovril, her facial paralysis more evident than ever. Margaret Rossiter went across to the bed, lifted up the mug and took a sip herself.

'It tastes perfectly all right to me, but I can easily get another mug if you'd prefer it.'

'What's one little sip? It's just as I thought; you'll only pour this one away and then you'll try again in some other way.'

The young nurse had had enough. Although the meat extract was much stronger than she liked and did seem rather bitter, she drained the mug and put it back on the tray with a loud thump.

'There, perhaps that will convince you. Now, do you want me to send for another cup and some marmalade, or not?'

Penny Craven seemed to have lost interest; she lay back on the pillows and stared at the ceiling, totally ignoring the nurse and the maid who came up to collect the tray. Margaret Rossiter settled back in the easy chair and when her patient showed no signs of wanting to talk, got out her knitting and concentrated on the complicated pattern.

★ ★ ★

Penny Craven had to wait for fifteen minutes before she was quite certain that the drugs were going to work, then she saw the nurse's eyelids begin to droop and her head suddenly fell forwards. The young woman came to again with a start, tried to pick up the two stitches she had dropped, shook her head as if to try to clear it and then slumped back in the chair. A couple of minutes later she was fast asleep, breathing heavily.

Penny was hopelessly out of condition, desperately underweight and still suffering from the effects of all the drugs she had been given, but somehow she managed to find the strength to heave the unconscious nurse on to the bed and undress her completely. All the clothes were too big for her, but at least everything was clean and when she tightened the belt around the uniform dress and pulled up the tights hard, she felt that at least she looked fairly presentable. The shoes were at least three sizes too large, but that was better than having them too small, and when she had blocked in the toes with wool, they were even reasonably comfortable. There was absolutely nothing she could do about her face, but provided she made no attempt to smile, even that wasn't all that obvious.

She put the night-shirt on the unconscious nurse, tucked her up neatly and after picking up the shoulder bag, opened the door a crack and looked down the corridor. She breathed a sigh of relief when she saw that it was deserted and walked down to the next floor, found a lavatory and sat on the seat, her head between her knees, trying to fight off the spasm of faintness that was threatening to overcome her.

When her heart had stopped thumping

and she felt a little better, she glanced at the nurse's watch. It was a few minutes after nine and she calculated that at best she would have two hours before they discovered her absence. She was quite sure that their first move would be to telephone her husband and she had to get there before they did.

She found three pound-notes and some loose change in the nurse's purse — at least that would be one fewer problem, being just enough for her needs. Luck had been with her so far and with so many agency nurses about, she did not anticipate any difficulty in getting out, but, even so, she was in a constant state of anxiety unil she was sitting on the top deck of the bus on the way to central London.

The journey took her a good deal longer than she had anticipated and by the time she had reached her destination, she was shaking uncontrollably. Unless she managed to steady herself up, she knew that she would never be able to go through with it and although she was only too well known in the local off licence, that was a risk she was going to have to run.

'Only half a bottle, Mrs. Craven?'

The man was laughing at her behind that bland façade; she knew it with utter and complete certainty. He was laughing at her ridiculous dress, her deformed face and above all at her pathetic dependence on that colourless liquid, but just for once she wasn't going to rise to the bait and spoil everything.

'Yes, thank you, that's all I need for today — you needn't bother to wrap it.'

The man knew that she was going to drink it as soon as possible — she could tell that from his expression — but it was long past the time to be worrying about little things like that and she hurried out, walked briskly across the road and in through the main entrance to the block of flats. Once in the safety of the telephone booth and when she felt the familiar warmth of the raw spirit in her stomach, her pulse rate settled, her sweating attack subsided and the shake in her hands began to diminish, ceasing completely within a few minutes.

On one never to be forgotten occasion a

few months earlier Penny had locked herself out of the flat when in urgent need of a drink, the caretaker with the master-key had been out at the time and she had had to wait for Mike to return. She had made a feeble attempt to hide the half empty vodka bottle, which she had carelessly left on the table in the sitting room, but of course he had seen it and the incident had started yet another round of bitter wrangling and mutual accusation. Soon after that, she had hidden a spare key under the wall to wall carpeting in the corridor where one of the tacks was loose and to her relief it was still there.

Even if Mike was out, she thought the chances of her being able to wait there with impunity until he returned were good; surely no one would think of looking for her there. She eased the key into the lock, gently pushed the door open and stepped inside.

★ ★ ★

Craven was feeling utterly drained by the time he had driven Claire back to

London. He deliberately avoided using the road where Carlo had crashed in case the police were there and the diversion added half an hour to their journey. The breakfast and the two cups of strong black coffee, which they had on their way back, revived him to some extent, but while Claire was having her burn dressed properly at the City Hospital, the familiar smell and surroundings brought back all the problems he still had to face.

Claire was still looking pale and drawn when they got back to her flat and he insisted that she went to bed with a sleeping pill.

'Why don't you join me?'

'Perhaps I will later on — I just want to think things over for a bit first.'

'Why not leave it until after you've had a sleep?'

'I don't think I'd be able to get off at the moment.'

'Don't take it so hard, Mike — you couldn't help Carlo's death.'

Carlo's death hadn't been on Craven's mind at all, but he wasn't going to admit that to Claire.

'Perhaps you're right.' He bent down to kiss her. 'I'll come in before too long, don't worry.'

'Mike,' she called softly when he had reached the door, 'thanks.'

Craven sat down on the sofa and to try to take his mind off Penny and what he was going to do about her, went over the whole business once more. There would be nothing at the scene of the crash to suggest that Carlo's death had been anything other than an accident and with the gun being, he was quite sure, the one that the young Italian had used to shoot Barrett, the murder and Carlo's subsequent flight would all tidily be explained.

He didn't think that Bert or any of the people at the hotel would present any problems either; now, with Carlo and Barrett out of the way, they would no doubt drift off into other nefarious activities and he didn't see why he or Claire should get involved with the police — the complications would be endless.

When he went back to the bedroom, Claire was sleeping peacefully and he decided to go back to his own flat, deal

243

with any mail and pick up some clean clothes. He heard the phone ringing as he walked along the corridor, but he had some difficulty with the door on account of the pile of circulars on the floor and was still a few paces short of the instrument when it fell silent.

Probably a wrong number, he thought, and sat back in the easy chair, looking around and realising just how shabby and dirty the place had become. Would he really be able to leave Penny and would Claire want him if he did? He sat there for a good half hour and was nearer to a solution to his problems at the end of that time. Finally, he got wearily to his feet and reached for the telephone; it was an index of how little he had been thinking about Penny when he discovered that he had forgotten the number of the nursing home and he started to search for it in the directory, only to be interrupted by a sharp ring on the door-bell.

Craven's surprise at seeing Enrico Morruzzi standing there was so complete that he just remained where he was, his mouth hanging open.

'Aren't you going to invite me in?'

The heavily built man with the iron-grey hair walked slowly into the hall, took off his brown light-weight overcoat and led the way back into the living room. He motioned to Craven to sit down on the sofa and took the chair from behind the desk and settled himself in front of the door. Once seated, he removed his right hand from the pocket of his jacket and the snub-nosed automatic looked like a toy in the man's massive fist.

'I'm going to kill you, Mr. Craven, but before I do, I want you to know why. Loyalty is a strange thing and one can find it in unexpected people. You made a bad mistake when you killed Barrett, you know, Mr. Craven. You see, when Bert Francis found Carlo in his car, he went back to the house, discovered his friend shot dead in the bedroom and rang me up straight away; I was waiting outside Mrs. Markham's flat when you returned and then followed you here.

'I might just possibly have given you the benefit of the doubt over Carlo's crash, although I know about you, Mr.

Craven, and you would have had the skill to run him off the road, but you shouldn't have left the gun in the car and tried to pin Barrett's murder on him. Perhaps you don't understand how much I prize the family name, but you soon will. I am seventy-five, Mr. Craven, I served my apprenticeship in the United States fifty years ago and I know what it is to act decisively; I have nothing against Mrs. Markham personally, but she is also going to have to die, just as you are.'

Craven heard a sharp click, which came from the direction of the hall, followed by the creak of a board. Morruzzi appeared not to have noticed anything and continued to speak almost as if to himself.

'I knew that Barrett and Francis worked for Carlo and I'm not so blind that I failed to realise that a lot of their activities were illegal, but my nephew was young and I thought that in time he would become more responsible. He always was a bit wild — that's why my brother sent him over to me — but he would have grown out of it, had he been given the opportunity. He was so full of life and to be cut off like that . . . ' The tears began to roll down the old man's cheeks.

While Morruzzi had been speaking, Craven had been inching his right hand towards the heavy glass ash-tray, which was sitting on the arm of the sofa; someone was creeping along the corridor outside and he only needed the old Italian to be distracted for a second or two.

Behind Morruzzi, the door slowly began to come open and Craven saw Penny standing there. He was so utterly taken aback that he could only sit there staring at her in amazement. She looked pale and ill, her hair was all over the place and the ludicrous dress she was wearing hung in folds across her thin shoulders. She obviously hadn't seen the gun and Morruzzi still didn't appear to have heard anything. Craven made frantic signals with his eyes to try to get Penny to leave, tensing himself at the same time and getting an even firmer grip on the ash-tray.

'Mike! Mike, I . . . '

Craven would never have believed that a man of Morruzzi's age could have moved so fast. Even though he hurled the ash-tray at the very second that the old Italian whirled round, he was far too late. The automatic jerked in his hand and the next instant the heavy implement took him on the back of the head, landing with a sickening thud, and the man fell sideways on to the floor.

Penny was lying in a crumped heap on the carpet by the door and Craven knelt down beside her, gently turned her over and cradled her head on his lap. The bullet had taken her full in the chest and he knew at once that it was hopeless; her lips were already turning blue and when she gave a little choking cough, a thin streak of blood coursed down her chin.

'Mike,' she whispered, her voice almost inaudible, 'who is he?'

'A madman. He was going to kill me and you saved my life.'

'I'm glad. I'm finished, Mike and I'm glad about that, too.'

'Don't say that, Penny. You'll be all right.'

The ghost of a smile crossed her face. 'You never were a good liar.' She closed her eyes and he thought for a moment that she had gone, but then she opened them again and miraculously her voice was even a little stronger when she spoke. 'They wouldn't let me see you at the nursing home and that's why I had to get away. You see, I have something very important to tell you, Mike.'

'Don't worry yourself now, love. Just lie there quietly and I'll phone for an ambulance.'

'No, Mike, it's too late now and what I have to say is really important. You see, you weren't driving when we had that crash — I was. Although you didn't realise it, I was a hopeless alcoholic long before the accident and somehow managed to keep it from you. That evening before we left, I told myself that I would have one last one, just for the road, and it was the last straw — I took a stupid risk and the car couldn't take the bend. I was badly cut about the face in the crash, but otherwise not seriously hurt and it sobered me up; I pulled you clear and told the police that you had been driving. I banked on you being too confused to remember the journey clearly, but it was made easy for me when you proved to be totally amnesic for it. I know what it has done to you, Mike; I'm so ashamed and so sorry — I never had the courage to tell you before.'

'Don't worry, my love — I understand.'

Another little smile crossed her face. 'I really believe you do.'

He continued to hold her pathetically wasted body in his arms long after she had died and all the pent up emotion of the last year exploded. He cried as he had never cried in his life before and half an hour after it was over, he was still sitting there, rocking her gently back and forth. When the telephone rang, he laid her down and, as if in a dream, walked across the room and lifted the receiver.

'Mr. Craven?'

'It's McAlister here — thank God I've found you. I've been trying to get you for a couple of hours. Your wife managed to get away from the building somehow — we're still searching for her, but if she has got right away, I fear she may try to harm you . . . ' Craven had an insane desire to laugh. 'Mr. Craven! Are you still there?'

'Yes, I'm here, Dr. McAlister, and so is Penny. She never meant me any harm.'

'Why didn't you ring me, man? We've had the staff searching for . . . '

Craven gently replaced the receiver. Five minutes later, he was still standing there, staring out of the window.

THE END

We do hope that you have enjoyed reading this large print book.

Did you know that all of our titles are available for purchase?

We publish a wide range of high quality large print books including:
Romances, Mysteries, Classics
General Fiction
Non Fiction and Westerns

Special interest titles available in large print are:
The Little Oxford Dictionary
Music Book, Song Book
Hymn Book, Service Book

Also available from us courtesy of Oxford University Press:
Young Readers' Dictionary
(large print edition)
Young Readers' Thesaurus
(large print edition)

For further information or a free brochure, please contact us at:
Ulverscroft Large Print Books Ltd.,
The Green, Bradgate Road, Anstey,
Leicester, LE7 7FU, England.
Tel: (00 44) **0116 236 4325**
Fax: (00 44) **0116 234 0205**

THE DAY OF MURDER

Brian Bearshaw

The body had been there a week before it was discovered. Detective Superintendent Townley and Sergeant Newman have a houseful of suspects. But who savagely killed the promiscuous woman in her flat? The time of death is narrowed to a few hours on the Sunday morning, which points to the only visitor to the house at that time — the parish priest. Yet there are eight suspects in total . . . and Townley and Newman will identify the guilty party before the day is out.

THE WOLVES

Lawrence Williams

A war in which men die in great numbers in mud-filled trenches is regarded with loathing. Yet often the same people justify the actions of small bands of men who fight behind enemy lines. These men are rarely depicted as vicious and brutal. Instead, they are considered daring, surmounting incredible odds and hardships: should one of them be fatally wounded, unselfishly he will stay behind to hold up the pursuing enemy . . . In fact, the reality is somewhat different.

NIGHTMARE FOR DR. MORELLE

Ernest Dudley

Helping Interpol unmask the big wheel behind an international narcotics racket, Dr. Morelle himself becomes involved in a train smash, with unforeseen results. Meanwhile, Miss Frayle, his querulous and inimitable secretary, makes a flying dash across the Continent to help him — but is also caught up in the sinister tangle.

THE GLOWING MAN

John Russell Fearn

Under the cover of darkness and a violent storm, electrical engineer Sidney Cassell thought he'd committed the perfect murder. But immediately after pushing his rival to his death from atop a pylon, he himself is struck by a live high-voltage cable. Cassell survives the accident, only to discover that the electrical shock has affected his body strangely ... Soon he becomes sucked into a vortex of murders and treachery, hunted by the police and unscrupulous scientists seeking the secret of his weird affliction.

THE WHISTLING SANDS

Ernest Dudley

Along with a large cash legacy, Miss Alice Ames had inherited the Whistling Sands, an old house overlooking the Conway Estuary. And it was here she began married life with Wally Somers — alias Wally Sloane, wanted by the Sydney police. To Wally, Alice and the Whistling Sands were just a means to the money he stood to gain. But when both had come to mean more to him than that, he became enmeshed in a web of deceit — and murder . . .

PLACE MILL

Barbara Softly

In 1645, the Civil War rages and
young Nicholas Lambert joins the
Royalist Army, leaving his sister
Katharine behind. Six years later,
with the Royalists defeated, Nicholas
is a fugitive. Returning home for
safety, accompanied by two friends,
he finds much has changed. Taking
Katharine and his cousin Hester as
cover, they attempt to escape to
France, but encounter difficulties
before even reaching the coast. And
then Katharine disappears . . . Suspi-
cious of their new acquaintances, who
will they be able to trust?